BEAGLES LOVE MUFFIN BUT MURDER

A SMALL TOWN CULINARY COZY MYSTERY

BEAGLE DINER COZY MYSTERIES

C. A. PHIPPS

For my son who is everything I hoped he would become.
Strong, loving, clever and caring.
We are richer for having you in our lives. xx

CONTENTS

BEAGLES LOVE MUFFIN BUT MURDER

Muffin but clues and criminals!
When the unthinkable happens—another murder, ex-celebrity chef Lyra St. Claire is once more hounded by the paparazzi.
The sheriff doesn't appreciate her help, but how can she carry on as if nothing's happened? To make matters worse, her new server is causing problems at the diner and the entire staff are on edge.
Her beagle, Cinnamon, sniffs out more than muffins and Lyra has to make a choice between family and friends when love is in the air.

Will she solve the crime before the paparazzi make her worst fears come true?

Beagle Diner Cozy Mysteries are light and entertaining, with a cornucopia of clues, delicious baking and a one clever beagle.

You'll find a great recipe at the end of the book! □

Beagle Diner Cozy Mysteries

Beagles Love Cupcake Crimes

Beagles Love Steak Secrets

Beagles Love Muffin But Murder

Beagles Love Layer Cake Lies

Join my newsletter to receive the bonus epilogue and new releases!

1

There was something about muffins that spoke of comfort food and love. Spread with butter or left as they were, all flavors were filling and delicious. Of course, Lyra St. Claire, ex-celebrity chef, might be biased.

She stood back to admire the glass cabinet full of today's baking, her eye drawn to the counter where a covered dish held large savory muffins. Fresh from the oven, her customers hadn't spied them yet, and she anticipated a variety of feedback. Not that she'd had any complaints about her food so far, but the diner in small-town Fairview didn't operate the same way as her LA restaurant had.

The truth was some dishes were never going to be a hit here. Plain and tasty won hands down over fancy, but that wouldn't stop her from pushing the boundaries from time to time. The thought amused her since a muffin could hardly be considered "out there."

No longer a celebrity chef, at least in her eyes, she'd settled into her new life easily. Well, easy might be an exaggeration. She missed the vibe of a restaurant kitchen from time to time, but it wasn't that causing issues. Unfortunately, a murder and several dramas along the way to solving it had given her many sleepless nights. She wiped her hands down her apron and shook her head. That was all behind her, and Lyra was determined to focus on the happiness the move home to Fairview brought with it.

"What's that grin for?" Her assistant poured two coffees from the machine at the end of the counter.

"I'm thinking that despite everything that's happened since we arrived, I'm grateful we made the move here. What about you?"

How Maggie and the others felt mattered a great deal to Lyra. Life was far different for the three people who followed her to the small town near Portland. She wanted her friends and family to be as happy as she was with their change in circumstances. Personal assistant, Maggie, along with Dan, her handyman and ex-driver, as well as her mom, took a huge leap of faith in coming here from the hustle and bustle of LA. It would be awful if they had regrets.

"Don't talk crazy." Maggie handed her one of the coffees. "I love working for you. Life is never dull, and I'm proud that your latest cookbook is doing so well—with my input."

Lyra laughed and would have hugged her if the hot coffees weren't a deterrent. She took the cup, grateful for the caffeine fix as well as their friendship. The first because she had been up early to get some cooking and baking underway before the breakfast rush, and the second, because without Maggie she would surely have found the transition from big to small town a lot tougher. Growing up here was not the same as owning a business, and having a colorful past some couldn't forget was at times awkward.

Breakfast rush over, the diner always had a few customers who stayed for as long as they liked. This included the Fairview knitting club, who sat at their usual table.

Due to a strange set of circumstances, Vanessa Fife, the mother of Lyra's last server, Poppy, and the previous unofficial leader of this boisterous group, was now a member of staff here. Her inability to give the group much time due to her job paved the way for Carrie-Ann to slip into the role. Usually good-natured, Carrie-Ann was enjoying this unexpected elevation in status, and her voice rang throughout the room, which made Lyra smile. How Vanessa felt about it could be seen in the lines around her mouth.

Earl Crane, the dishwasher, somberly cleared tables and attempted to keep away from the group who had a knack for teasing him mercilessly. The poor young man had enough to contend with. He'd lost his good friend, and fellow worker, when Poppy pleaded guilty to the recent murder and arson. None of them had suspected her, and Lyra sighed at the odd turn of events that had Poppy's mom working here instead. Life sure could change in an instant, and often in ways you could never predict.

Did it make Lyra more wary of hiring going forward? Heck, yes! She'd needed more staff, and no matter that Maggie helped when necessary, this was not what she'd been employed for. So, when Vanessa pleaded her case of no income and no knowledge of what her daughter was up to, Lyra didn't have the heart to refuse. Not many people could understand why Lyra would give her a chance, but so far Vanessa had kept her toned-down manner relatively free from the terseness she was known for.

"Yoo-hoo! Lyra!" Carrie-Ann beckoned her over.

"Sorry, I was miles away."

"Thinking about that man of yours?" Carrie-Anne's eyebrows did a fascinating mambo. "I bet you're missing him already."

The only person Carrie-Anne could be referring to was Lyra's good friend, who ran his restaurant in Portland. "Kaden? No, I was thinking about how great it is to be back home and have things return to normal around here."

"Bless you, and thank goodness you did come back and sort out the diner before it was demolished. We can't imagine being anywhere else now. Can we, ladies?"

The others agreed, and Lyra smiled. She'd meant that she was glad to be back from her week's holiday to see her friend Kaden and wasn't referring to the spring day she'd arrived in Fairview. Carrie-Ann often skipped between topics, so Lyra let it slide. "That's lovely to hear. How was the muffin?"

Carrie-Ann rolled her eyes. "Heaven on a plate. I'd never think to put all those savory ingredients together, and it was so filling."

"I'm glad you think so."

"Only it does cause a conundrum."

"Oh?"

Carrie-Anne's eyes twinkled. "I saw the sweet ones you just put out, but I have no room to try one."

Lyra laughed at the fake problem. "The banana ones? Why not take one home for later?"

"What a good idea. Please box one up so I don't miss out. Where is your mom this morning?"

"She had an errand to run."

Carrie-Ann tilted her head. As leader of the group, she might be more pleasant than Vanessa, but she was no less inquisitive about the happenings in town. Lyra merely smiled and collected the empty plates. What her mom was up to didn't concern anyone else.

"I don't see Vanessa around either. How's she doing? Does she mention Poppy at all?"

Lyra's smile slipped. The mere mention of the young waitress still upset her, and she wasn't inclined to discuss her newest staff member either. "As far as I know, everyone is well. Vanessa will be in later. Why don't you ask her then?"

Carrie-Ann pouted. "She's a little closemouthed about it all."

"I imagine she needs some time to deal with everything. This is a very difficult situation, as I'm sure you can imagine."

Martha Curran, her mom's best friend, frowned. "Isn't that what we just talked about, Carrie-Ann—giving Vanessa some space?"

Carrie-Ann pouted some more. "Sure, but she is my friend, and I want her to know that I'm here if she needs to talk."

"I'm sure she knows how we feel." With a shake of her head, Martha turned back to Lyra. "Vanessa did mention that you were hiring again."

"I've been looking into it and started running ads a couple of days ago. In fact, I have a couple of people coming for interviews today."

"That's good news." Martha smiled. "With the summer festival about to kick off, you'll need all the help you can get."

Lyra nodded. "I remember from when I used to live here how it attracted a lot of out-of-towners."

"I'm sure having a celebrity in our midst will attract far more this time," Carrie-Ann said importantly.

"People will have forgotten about my show by now." Lyra gently dismissed the notion.

"Don't be modest, dear." Carrie-Anne waved a dismissive hand. "Your show is still on. We watch the reruns, don't we, ladies?"

The group nodded as one, hanging on every word while their fingers automatically did clever things to the various garments they were knitting.

Esther Rand, gray-haired and sweet, giggled. "I've been trying one of the recipes, but the show goes too fast, and I'm pretty sure I missed something because it didn't look the same at all."

"Then don't penny-pinch and buy her cookbooks," Martha tutted.

Lyra bit back a laugh at the shock on Esther's face. She was particularly careful with her money, but perhaps it was out of necessity. She really didn't know many people well yet, and most of the ones she'd gone to school with had left town or she hadn't bumped into again. However, this group were as close to unpaid cheerleaders as a person could get, and it wouldn't hurt to know more about them. "Tell me which one you'd like to make, Mrs. Rand, and I'll see if I can't hunt out the recipe for you."

Esther grinned. "How sweet of you. That would be wonderful."

"Excuse me. I'm sorry to interrupt, Ms. St. Claire."

They turned to face a tall woman with short fair hair. The regulars usually took a seat unless they wanted something from the cabinet or a coffee to take away. This woman wasn't one of them, and since no one recognized her, was probably a visitor to town. Lyra had seen her studying the special board on the counter and hoped she hadn't been waiting too long.

She excused herself to the group. "Sorry to keep you waiting. Would you like to take a seat?"

The woman glanced at the interested faces behind Lyra and lowered her voice. "I'm not here as a customer. It's about the job."

Checking her watch, Lyra saw that time had flown this morning. "Are you Raylene Dwyer?"

"That's right. I hope I'm not too early?" Her voice dipped considerably while her knuckles whitened on the handbag she clutched.

Interviewing for anything new made everyone nervous, and having an audience didn't help. Lyra deliberately ignored the group in favor of putting Raylene at ease. There would be plenty of time to introduce a new employee later—if she was satisfactory. "Not at all, early is always better than late. Come out the back where we can talk privately."

The applicant nodded enthusiastically.

"Please take a seat in the office. There's some paperwork to fill out on the desk which you can make a start on." Lyra showed her to the door, then turned to speak to her assistant who sat at the large kitchen table. "Maggie, could you take care of the diner while I'm interviewing, please?"

"Sure." Maggie glanced at the large clock above her. "She's keen," she added softly on her way past.

Half an hour to be precise, which Lyra chose to take as a good sign. Inside the office, Raylene sat primly on the edge of her chair, filling out the forms. Up close, Lyra decided she was perhaps a few years older than herself–possibly midthirties. Neatly dressed, her hands were clean, with short nails. There were dark smudges under her blue eyes that a heavy layer of concealer barely hid. Perhaps nerves to start over at a new job had kept her awake.

Lyra remembered times like that. When she was new to her cooking class and then the show that was now canceled, she'd hardly slept a wink. But this wasn't the time for reflections, and she consulted her notes. "I see you've had waitressing experience."

Raylene nodded. "Yes, I worked for a large diner in Portland. It was a while ago."

"And you've been traveling ever since, though you live in Fairview now?"

The woman nodded. "I rented a house last week. It's a couple of blocks away."

"That is handy." Being able to walk to work was certainly a plus. There'd be no excuses of cars breaking down or other transport issues.

"When I saw you were hiring, I couldn't believe my luck that I'd live close to work." Raylene blushed. "I mean, if I got the job."

Lyra already liked the woman, who wasn't pushy, but clearly eager for the position. Gun-shy after an employee failure, she'd gambled desperately on Vanessa, who had turned out well—so far. "Let's tick off a few more things first. Your resume says you can work a coffee machine and a register. Plus, you've used tablets to take orders before?"

Raylene nodded enthusiastically. "I came early to see how your diner operates and believe I have all the necessary skills. I don't mind hard work. In fact, I like to be busy and will take any hours you offer."

While she didn't want to rush into this, Lyra had a good feeling. "I prefer to start early, so I'd like to have someone who can start later and work later. The main reason is so I can walk my dog. She's a beagle who loves attention, and you'll see her hanging around the back veranda."

"That would suit me fine, and I love dogs!" Raylene grinned.

This was what she needed to hear. Raylene's last reference was glowing and had been verified by Maggie yesterday. She certainly looked good on paper. Lyra took the forms and checked that everything was filled in. When she saw that all the tax and bank information was done, she looked up and nodded in satisfaction. So much for taking her time. "In that case, when can you start?"

Raylene gulped. "Really? How about tomorrow?"

"Wonderful. If you've got time now, I'll show you around and introduce you to the staff that are here."

"I have all day, and I'm in no hurry."

Lyra couldn't have been more delighted by this flexibility. Business was booming, and they were short-staffed. Raylene was exactly what the diner needed, and the ability to start right away couldn't be more perfect. She showed her the kitchen first. "This is Leroy. He's our head cook and in charge when I'm not here or my mom. Raylene will be starting work tomorrow."

Leroy gave the woman a once-over and smiled, though it was a little forced. "Welcome aboard."

"Thank you," Raylene said softly and looked away.

Did she know about Poppy? And did it matter if she did? Raylene was here, and the diner certainly needed her. While it might seem that Leroy's welcome was a little cool, Lyra empathized. He'd been very attached to Poppy as her mentor and friend. Naturally, he was wary of befriending a newcomer so soon. Just like Earl, who was almost inside the dishwasher as if trying to hide.

"This is Earl. He's our head dishwasher, but also helps in the diner clearing tables and delivering orders."

"Hello, Earl."

"Ma'am." Earl nodded shyly.

Maggie came to collect an order.

"And this is Maggie. She's my assistant and is supposed to be working on other things, but kindly pitches in when necessary. She'll be just as glad to have you here as the rest of us—maybe more so."

Maggie laughed. "I don't mind working in the diner. Although preferably not full-time."

Lyra laughed at the honesty and showed Raylene around the kitchen. "Let's go take a proper look at the diner."

They stopped at the counter to where the huge coffee machine sat, followed by the register. "As you probably know, a coffee machine like this is worth its weight in gold. Would you mind giving me a demonstration of your ability?" It had taken Vanessa

12

a long time to work the machine, which had been the only downside so far to hiring her.

Raylene nodded and washed her hands before commencing. "How about a mocha?"

"Perfect. They're Maggie's favorites and can make her day."

Raylene was fast and exact. With a flourish of fresh espresso over a heaped teaspoon of ganache in a cup, she mixed them together, then poured the hot milk over it, leaving a good froth that magically portrayed a leafy pattern. Something Lyra had never mastered. Next, Raylene held a saucer over half the cup and sprinkled grated chocolate on the exposed half, then placed the cup on a clean saucer and handed the mocha to Lyra. Taking a step back, Raylene clasped her hands in front of her.

"It looks and smells great." Lyra took a tentative sip. "Mmmm. Delicious and just the right temperature. Maggie will be thrilled. Just a heads up, our customers are slowly coming around to the fancier kind, but regular coffee is still a staple, and those cups should always be refilled. The tablets are used for every ordered item and sends a ticket to the kitchen for whoever is cooking to work from. Depending on the day or time, that could be me, my mom, or Leroy."

Raylene didn't hesitate. "I'm familiar with ordering that way and know how much faster they are than writing up a docket which might be misread—and it saves a few trees in the process."

"Exactly." The longer they spent together, the more positive Lyra felt about hiring her. "Do you have any questions?"

"Not right now. Maybe when I start, I might think of something?" She said this almost apologetically.

"Of course. No question is a silly one, so please don't hesitate to ask any of us for help until you get your bearings and even afterward. You'll have a small locker near the office for your bag and a peg for your apron. You can choose a hot meal every day you work, no charge, and there's a staff discount on everything else. My mom comes in to help in the mornings, and I'm looking at hiring some casual staff for the summer festival in a few weeks. Times may change depending on who I hire and what their experience is, but for now, if you could come in at 10:00 a.m. tomorrow, we'll get you started. By the way, I mentioned Cinnamon before. She's very friendly, incredibly nosey, and is not allowed in the diner or kitchen. I'd rather you didn't feed her and please discourage customers if you can do so politely." Lyra grimaced. "Unfortunately, my dog never refuses food."

Raylene nodded. "It makes sense to have some control over her diet. I guess it's hard for your customers to refuse her when she's such a sweetie."

"You're right; they think they're being kind and that no one will notice a tidbit, but they all add up over the course of a day." Lyra shook her head at that, wondering at the same time if Raylene had seen Cinnamon when she'd scoped out the diner earlier. This was another tick for her new employee, proving how thorough she was. "I think that's it for now. Any questions?"

"None that I can think of. Thank you so much for this opportunity," Raylene gushed. "I think the diner is wonderful and can't wait to start. See you in the morning."

She'd barely breezed out the front door when Carrie-Ann caught Lyra's eye. The waving arms couldn't be ignored, and really there was no point now that the decision was made. "She starts tomorrow, and her name's Raylene."

"Such a pretty name, and she looked so happy by the time she left. Fingers crossed she doesn't let you down," Carrie-Ann added.

Martha tutted. "That couldn't happen twice."

A breeze came through the door, along with Officer Walker. *Surely it was only the breeze making her* *shiver.*

2

Tall and handsome, with short brown hair and cool gray eyes, Sheriff Walker was impressive in uniform—and not too shabby out of it. Lyra's cheeks flamed as if she'd voiced the thought aloud. Heaving a sigh of relief when no one reacted, she shook her head at the silliness. Naturally, she'd been innocently thinking of him in jeans and a T-shirt.

"Good morning, Sheriff," the knitting group chorused.

"Ladies." He removed his hat, nodded, then switched his attention to Lyra and followed her to the counter. "The usual, please."

Without hesitation she slipped a fresh muffin into a bag while Maggie made his coffee. Naturally the sheriff noticed.

"Ahhh, what did you put in there?" He pointed at the bag.

"A muffin," she said casually and picked up another bag.

Confusion took a few years off his usually stern features. "Is it for me? Because I wanted a cupcake."

She almost laughed. "You can have one of those as well. I want an honest opinion on these new savory muffins and thought you'd be my best bet. Do you mind? It's free."

Rob McKenna, a neighbor and friend, had been her go-to person for honest feedback outside of Maggie and Dan. With his death, the unpaid job was vacant. Where the spontaneous decision to ask him to step into the large shoes came from, she wasn't entirely sure. He blinked a couple of times, and she thought he might refuse.

"I guess it's okay. What's in it?" he asked suspiciously.

"Good things, like spinach, feta, and pine nuts."

His face screwed up comically. "What the heck? I hate spinach."

"You sound like a big baby." She smirked. "I promise it's not the kind that you've probably eaten before—all mushed up and soggy. Anyway, you're used to tackling things you don't like, so why not give it a try. Like I said, it's free."

He peered into the bag and grimaced. "Free isn't much of an incentive if it makes me gag."

"I should be offended, and if you didn't look so scared, I might have been. Tell me when you've had anything here that made you gag?"

"There's a first time for everything."

"Suit yourself." She shrugged and held her hand out. "Don't have it, but I swear you'll be sorry you missed out on such a tasty muffin."

He raised an eyebrow, and Maggie laughed.

"Lyra's not fooling. They're delicious."

"If other people have already tried them," he huffed, "why do you need me to eat one?"

"Because Maggie loves everything I bake, where as I know you'll be brutally honest. I need that when I'm contemplating putting a new recipe in one of my cookbooks."

"So, I'm your guinea pig?" He groaned and held the bag as if it contained poison. "Twist my arm then—since it's for research."

When Lyra simply grinned he shook his head. "How do you do that?"

"I don't know what you mean, Sheriff," she said innocently.

He snorted. "You get people to do exactly what you want even when they don't want to."

"Me? I wish that were true."

"Hmmph!" He swiped his card while his lips fought against a smile.

On the way out he passed Dan. They looked each other up and down and nodded. The two had a strange relationship, which had begun when Walker suspected Dan of killing Rob McKenna, who he was boarding with at the time. They'd called a truce and obviously respected each other, but some things stuck and were clearly hard to get over.

"What would you like, Dan?"

He looked up at the board above their heads to check today's specials. "Chicken fettuccine sounds good. It's such a nice day and I could use a break, so I'll eat it out on the veranda."

"I can put that through," Vanessa offered.

"Thank you." Lyra hadn't seen her arrive and appreciated the way Vanessa didn't muck around when she was at work. She'd be the perfect person to walk Raylene through her paces after her induction, and Lyra'd ask her about it as soon as she could. Right now, there was something she wanted to discuss with Dan out of Maggie's and her mom's hearing, so she accompanied him down the small hall that joined the two dining spaces.

Cinnamon bounded across the wooden floor and slid to a stop at their feet. She loved everyone at the diner, but Dan and Maggie would always have a special place in the beagle's heart.

He immediately crouched and gave her a hug, then scratched her back the way she liked, talking to the beagle in the same sing-song voice everyone adopted when talking to pets.

"How was your holiday?" he asked eventually. "Are the press still hassling you?"

For weeks after the murder, the press hounded her relentlessly, making it hard to leave the farmhouse and harder still to get any work done in the diner. In the end Lyra took a week off and went to visit her friend Kaden Hunter in Portland. "Despite the reason, it was nice to get away, and thank goodness the fuss seems to have died… I mean, blown over."

He made a rude sound. "There's nothing like a murder to get them back on your tail, but hopefully they've given up trying to get an interview. How is Kaden?"

"Great. His restaurant's booming, and I forced him into letting me work a couple of shifts."

He snorted again. "Should I be surprised? As for 'forcing you,' it's more likely that he was only too happy to have the famous Lyra St. Claire work at Phoenix. I bet it's less crazy than the diner was while you were gone. Although, I daresay it was good for business?"

"Maggie told me the press hung around for a few more days until they realized I wasn't in town, and she also confirmed that sales were up. Unfortunately, poor Vanessa's had to cope with a few snide comments."

"It wasn't nice," he agreed. "Leroy, Maggie, and I ran as much interference as we could, but it was Arabelle, Martha, and Patricia who stood up to the press and almost ran them out of town."

Lyra chuckled at the image of three middle-aged women doing such a thing, and felt a rush of pride at the way the town circled wagons when one of their own was targeted.

They stood at the railing, away from a few customers who sat at the outside tables, looking down the parking lot to the hedge and beyond to Lyra's farmhouse with Cinnamon between them, ears perked and tail thumping the deck.

Over the tree tops to the left, Dan's garage and workshop roof could be seen. In fact, it was the rooftop of the apartment above that was visible.

"How's the garage doing?"

Dan was given the garage in Rob McKenna's will, and her former handyman was determined to make a go of it.

"Work is pretty steady, which is a relief." He grinned. "At the start people who know me from the diner were desperate enough to trust me with their vehicles rather than drive to Destiny or Portland. Since then, I guess the word got around that I do a good job, because I've had a lot of referrals and repeat customers."

"I'm so glad for you. Are you still working long hours?"

"Yep." He raised an eyebrow. "You know how that is."

She laughed. "I do, but I'm aiming to cut back in the future so I can do more testing."

"For a new book? Maggie says the last one's going great."

They'd known each other too long for there to be any caginess around her success. Besides, with the amount of time Dan and Maggie spent together, they were bound to discuss most things to do with the diner which Dan had refurbished. "It sold out twice, and they've had to do more print runs. Reviews are wonderful, but I do wonder how much of it is due to the drama around here."

"I guess some of the fever might have been, but a Lyra St. Claire cookbook is always hot property because the food is so darned good."

"You're certainly good for my self-esteem," she chuckled.

"I didn't realize you had a problem with that."

Maggie snorted from behind them. "Are you kidding? She's never understood why she's so famous." She pointed a finger at Lyra. "And don't say you aren't anymore and that you're only a diner owner these days, because the sales of that cookbook prove otherwise."

"Cut it out, you two. Cheerleading practice is done for the foreseeable future."

"It's the truth," Maggie protested.

They were interrupted as Lyra's mom brought out Dan's meal. "I hope this isn't your dinner, young man."

21

"No way. All this work means that I'm starving several times a day."

Back and forth, Patricia and Dan joked about how much he ate, and it seemed that Lyra wasn't going to get her private word with Dan after all. Since Patricia was back from her errands, Lyra excused herself and returned to her spreadsheets. In truth, it was Maggie who made the accounts balance, but after a harsh lesson running her LA restaurant, Lyra now signed off on everything.

Only her concentration was lagging. A good friend and huge part of Lyra's continued success, Maggie's happiness preyed on Lyra's ordered mind. Unfortunately, Dan was proving to be a block to this, and somehow she had to get him to understand why.

She'd been at it for half an hour when Patricia appeared at the door with Vanessa peering over her shoulder.

"Earl told us we have a new staff member starting tomorrow."

While Patricia was merely asking a question, Vanessa's forehead creased. This wasn't unusual, but Lyra wanted to reassure her, just in case it was perceived to be a threat.

"Sorry, I meant to tell you both sooner. To be honest, it was a quicker decision than I intended to make, and these accounts have been calling my name for a few days, so it slipped my mind when you arrived. Her name's Raylene, and I think she'll fit in well around here. She has plenty of experience, which will be a blessing with the festival coming up."

"Young or old?"

"Mom! You can't ask that of an employee these days, and it shouldn't matter."

Patricia shrugged. "Maybe not, but since it's just us here, did you form an opinion?"

Lyra hadn't checked the birth date on the paperwork, and she wasn't going to do so now. "Maybe midthirties—more importantly, I liked her."

"See, that wasn't so hard. Come on, Vanessa, let's leave her be. She gets grumpy when it's accounts time."

Lyra huffed, until she heard Patricia snicker, and then she chuckled too. After a rocky start when her mom moved into the farmhouse, they were getting on well. Therefore, a bit of good-natured ribbing was fine   with   her.

3

Next day, the breakfast rush was easing when Raylene, only fifteen minutes early this time, arrived at the back door with Cinnamon beside her. After a quick rap, she opened the screen door and stepped nervously inside.

"Welcome!" Lyra beckoned her closer. "You met everyone yesterday, except my mom, Patricia St. Claire, and Vanessa Fife, your fellow server."

Patricia was dropping cookie dough on a baking sheet that had circles printed onto it to ensure they would be uniform, and Vanessa literally had her hands full with an order to deliver.

"Pleased to meet you." Patricia waved sticky gloves. "We can get better acquainted when I'm done."

"Morning," Leroy called from the grill.

Raylene smiled weakly around the room.

"I'll be back in a minute." Vanessa hurried into the diner, her face a mask of neutrality.

Hopeful that this was a good sign, Lyra showed Raylene the small cubby to keep her bag, and then the shelf of aprons. "Please help yourself to a fresh one as often as necessary. Everyone should look clean when they go into the diner, whether you're serving behind the counter or taking orders."

Raylene nodded and tied on an apron. "It makes a much better impression than wearing a grubby one all day. These are very smart too."

Pleased with the comment, Lyra donned another and picked up a spare tablet. "I'll show you exactly how we do things, and as soon as you get the hang of it, let me know."

Vanessa reappeared, and seeing the wary glance she threw at Raylene, Lyra had a change of heart. "On second thoughts, I have a few things that need my attention. Vanessa will show you how the tablets work, then you can shadow her instead until you're comfortable. Is that okay with you, Vanessa?"

Two spots of color appeared on the older woman's cheeks. "I think understanding the way we do things is a good way to start."

Mom grinned over her trays of cookies, and Leroy gave Lyra a thumbs-up behind the other women's backs. It looked like they were on the same page. On occasion, Vanessa struggled to fit in, and being in charge in a small way might give her a boost of self-confidence she still lacked.

Before she'd gone to visit Kaden, Lyra worried that it was a huge mistake hiring Vanessa after all the trouble her daughter brought down on them. The girl was getting psychiatric help, but Vanessa had to live in the town where it all happened, and people had long memories. It couldn't be pleasant to have the topic brought up when she was trying to forget, or at least put it out of her mind as much as she could. Working in the diner must be a constant reminder that her daughter had not only inadvertently killed someone who was highly regarded but had hurt Leroy.

After feeling guilty for not seeing the extent of Poppy's problems, the main reason she'd given

Vanessa the job was so she could pay her mounting debts, and Lyra hadn't regretted the decision so far.

Lyra returned to her office, leaving the door open—she rarely closed it—so she could hear how the teaching progressed.

"You're picking that up quickly," Vanessa told Raylene. "There's the door chime; we better get out the front. I'll show you how we greet a new customer, and then you could probably try on your own for the next one."

"If you're sure." Raylene sounded nervous.

"I am," Vanessa said in that no-nonsense voice which had been missing for weeks.

With a sigh, Lyra went back to the accounts. Apart from the tone, it was positive encouragement and surely nothing to worry about. She'd barely looked at the first page when Maggie flounced into the office and flopped into a chair. "What's he done now?"

Maggie sniffed. "I don't know who you're talking about."

"A certain garage owner. He who can't say the right thing."

"Exactly! We were going on a picnic tonight, but the fool got a sudden booking he won't turn down. Apparently, it's urgent!"

"I've never considered Dan to be a liar."

"Your point is…?"

"Here's a thought. Maybe it is urgent."

Maggie groaned. "It's always urgent."

"You need to cut him a break. Dan just wants the business to work."

"I do his books, and let me tell you, it is working. Why can't he take it a little easier?"

"I think what you really mean is when is he going to make time for you? Am I right?"

Maggie groaned again. "Can't I just be annoyed for a while longer without you forcing me to be sensible and understanding?"

"Sure. Let me know when you're done." Lyra grinned. "You know the two of you are perfect together."

"Huh? I'm not sure about there being a perfect person—for anyone."

"My parents were, so I know it can happen," Lyra assured her. "You're so organized, compartmentalize well, and like Dan, you're always willing to help when a person needs you. Dan's also a hard worker, incredibly kind, and adores you. I think those traits complement each other."

Maggie rolled her eyes. "Don't make it weird, okay?"

"How is it weird that your talents could work in harmony? Plus, you look good together even when you're arguing." Lyra winked.

Black eyebrows knitted together. "I'll concede you might be right about that, but this is a new relationship and not at all serious."

Lyra snorted. Whether Maggie would admit it openly or not, they were a couple, and though her friend might argue about it, Lyra was sure that eventually she'd be reasonable because Maggie was the most practical person she knew. "Then why does it bother you so much when he changes your plans?"

"The word 'plan' says it all. You make them and you stick to them—end of story."

"If you truly thought like that, you never would have come to Fairview with me."

Maggie narrowed her eyes. "You're very good at twisting my words."

Seeing that Maggie wasn't ready to be sensible just yet, Lyra pulled a stack of papers toward her. "Perhaps I'll get back to my accounts."

When Maggie didn't move, Lyra looked up and smothered a grin. She could almost hear the gears turning as her friend digested their conversation. She wouldn't give in easily, but if that thoughtful look was anything to go by, Dan wasn't staying in the dog house for too long.

After a while, Maggie saw her watching and shook her head, then laughed. "Fine, I'll give him a little leeway."

"You won't regret it."

The eyebrows did a little dance. "Now, what about you and the sheriff?"

Lyra blinked. "That's a stretch too far. He's a lot friendlier, but I wouldn't even call us friends yet."

"I guess murder will slow down a romance."

"There is nothing like that in our future," Lyra insisted despite an odd swirling going on in the pit of her stomach when she thought of Walker, which she chose to put down to hunger pains—even though that was unlikely.

"Because of Kaden?" Maggie continued to prod.

Lyra groaned. "Not you too?"

"I know what you say, but as you admitted, I've never seen a man and a woman as close as you two and not have it turn into something."

"Well, you have now."

Maggie raised an eyebrow. "We've never discussed this, but surely you've considered that Kaden could be the one?"

Lyra smiled, remembering several times during their training when she had indeed thought that. They were as close as a man and woman could be, and he really understood her, but his friendship had been more important than a relationship at the time—and still was. Until recently, Maggie had only seen them during the difficult phase of their relationship, but they had an honest relationship, and it was a fair question. "I'd be lying if I said otherwise," she conceded. "The thing is, we weren't looking for more back then, and since we're both in agreement that what we have is amazing, we have no intention of now pushing for something that isn't there."

"Wow. I can't imagine having that conversation."

"It was sensible and necessary." Lyra stretched. "Now if you've finished interrogating me, I need to bake something."

"You'll have to check the accounts sooner or later." Maggie tipped her head at the computer.

Footsteps came from just outside the door, and they both looked that way, but no one appeared. Maybe whoever it was had changed their mind about interrupting. Sometimes, taking a moment or two to ponder an issue brought a solution.

Like Maggie and Dan. Or Kaden and Lyra.

4

Since yesterday's lot had sold out in record time, Lyra was making another batch of savory muffins the next morning, when Maggie dropped the local paper beside her on the counter. This was never a good sign. When there was good news about the diner, Maggie always read it loudly to the whole kitchen.

"I thought you might want to see this." Maggie tapped the front page and a recent photo of Lyra which was front and center.

"Despite a recent murder close to her diner and home, it's business as usual for Lyra St. Claire. The Beagle Diner, situated just outside Portland in Fairview, is owned and operated by the world-famous Celebrity Chef. The talk-show host and ex-LA restaurateur stepped down from her lofty heights to live behind her much smaller and less sophisticated business, trying to avoid more publicity around the scandals that plagued her career. Unfortunately, murder seems to be a permanent dish on her menu."

It went on in the same vein and rehashed the Portland murders from months ago. "Sheesh! This article makes it sound like I deliberately sought out places for murder to happen." She grimaced. "Or, more likely, that I'm the cause of them."

Shocked by her announcement, everyone in the kitchen stopped what they were doing.

Patricia read the article over Lyra's shoulder. "How they can be allowed to print this kind of rubbish?"

Maggie's lips thinned. "That's how the press is these days. Print what you like and hope no one challenges you over whether it's true or not; it seems to win over facts."

"Well, it's not good enough. I've a good mind to give the editor a ring. Once the locals get hold of the latest gossip, they'll be back in to hound us."

"I appreciate that, Mom, but it will blow over."

"Hmmm. We said that last time, and you had to run away to stop it."

"I didn't run." Lyra sniffed. "I took a much-needed break."

Patricia nodded. "Yes, of course you needed it, dear, but why was that, I ask?"

Leroy tapped his bell. "Sorry to break this up, but I have orders cooling here."

"I've got them." Raylene hurried by to collect a tray.

"She's a good worker," Patricia noted when she'd gone. "It's lucky you found her."

Thankful for the change of subject, Lyra smiled. "It sure is. I've been meaning to say that, as she's picked everything up so quickly, you should feel free to stop working here or drop your hours whenever you're ready."

"Are you sure?" Patricia tilted her head. "I'm happy to do as much as you need and help during the festival, but I would like to get back into the knitting group." She dropped her voice. "Let's give it a couple more days to make sure she's staying to be on the safe side."

Lyra almost dropped the tray of muffins she was carrying to the oven. "Why wouldn't Raylene stay? Did she say something?"

Patricia waved her hand. "I don't know. To be honest, she doesn't talk much about her personal life, and I wonder if there's more to moving here than a job opportunity."

"Like what? She told me that she was already here when she saw the job advertised."

"There you go. Maybe she has a husband or a beau in the background we don't know about and she's running away from them. She could be hiding out here."

The unspoken meaning that this was exactly what Lyra had done by coming home to Fairview when her career took its nose dive hung in the air. "Mom, she's only been working here for two days, and since it's none of our business, we should let her keep her reasons to herself," Lyra chided gently. "She'll tell us if she wants us to know."

"Naturally, I won't harass her for details." Patricia sniffed. "I just see her looking sad sometimes and wonder if she's lonely and missing friends and family."

Now that her mom mentioned it, Lyra had seen that sad look a few times. "I guess that's true for anyone who moves away from their home, but maybe we could help. Why don't you ask her to join us for a meal?"

Patricia grinned. "That sounds perfect. She might open up and stop being starstruck when she's near you. How about tonight?"

Her mom said the darndest things, but maybe she had a point about Raylene, who struggled to string two sentences together when Lyra was around. "Sure, as long as she has no other plans—I wouldn't like her to feel that she has to come if it would make her uncomfortable."

Patricia rolled her eyes. "I'll do my best not to make it sound that way."

"It wasn't a dig, Mom. I know you'll handle it perfectly." Pulling the muffins out of the oven, Lyra placed them on the cooling rack. "Can you put these out in a few minutes, please? I'm going to finish the accounts before I do anything else, otherwise Maggie will shoot me."

Lyra dropped the last piece of paper into the finished pile and sighed. Another month done! The diner was doing exceptionally well, and the stocktaking that Leroy did a few days ago indicated that all levels were exactly as they should be. Things seemed to have finally settled down, and her friends and family were happy.

Her glance fell on the paper Maggie had thrust into the bin by her desk. Someone was clearly intent on stirring up trouble again, but who? She checked the name—Lester Eckhart. As the owner of the paper, he'd introduced himself the day Lyra moved in, and when he realized she wasn't granting interviews on anything but the diner opening, and Dan escorted him off the premises, he didn't bother printing anything— good or bad. As far as she knew, and that was only through the knitting ladies, the paper had one other staff member, who was a woman. Having met the man, Lyra doubted that she could contribute anything to the paper if Mr. Eckhart didn't approve it first.

Maybe she should pay Mr. Eckhart a visit to find out why she was flavor of the day. Or should she leave it alone? Sometimes you could stir up a hornet's nest by reacting to needling articles.

Pushing back from her desk, she wandered out into the diner. There were several tables occupied, including the one the knitting group frequented most days. Vanessa and Raylene bustled about with coffee pots and took orders. Raylene was polite and smiled at each person as her fingers flew across the tablet. She repeated every order precisely just as Vanessa had schooled her.

"Hey, Lyra." Carrie-Anne waved her over to the group.

The group were consistent customers and mostly very sweet, if a little reliant on gossip to fill their day, and she always stopped by their table to show that their loyalty was appreciated by giving them some time, in the same way she had in her restaurant. "Good morning, ladies. How are you all?"

Carrie-Anne smiled warmly. "Wonderful, thank you. We like your new employee."

"I'm glad. She's doing well, isn't she?"

"She already knows what we like." Martha Curran winked. "Where is she from?"

"Why don't you ask her yourself? You know, give her a Fairview welcome, and get acquainted properly."

"That's a lovely idea. Maybe she could join us when she has a break," Carrie-Anne said thoughtfully.

The idea of the knitting group asking her questions had sprung from wanting to make Raylene feel part of the community. Now all Lyra could think of was giving up a lamb to slaughter. "Just be gentle. Raylene's a little shy."

Carrie-Anne huffed. "As if we would be anything else."

"I'll make sure she isn't given the third degree." Martha winked and received a glare from Carrie-Anne. "Although, it is nice to have some new blood in town."

Lyra gave a tight smile. While it wasn't her greatest idea, at least Raylene would be on a first-name basis with the women who knew everything about everyone. It would also provide conversation for tonight's dinner at the farmhouse. That pushed Lyra on to say a quick hi to her other regulars. Raylene had been shocked by the invite, according to Patricia, but pleased, and now Lyra had a menu to prepare. Nothing too fancy, but something Raylene might enjoy. Which was tricky since she hardly knew the woman.

She went into the chiller and found enough lean beef for five or six people. This would be perfect and easy to cook over at the farmhouse, which had a fantastic kitchen, but nothing like the diner's.

The whole concept of a dinner party appealed more with each minute. It would be just the family, which included herself, Patricia, Maggie, and Dan, plus Raylene. There was one more person she might invite, although it was very short notice so maybe he wouldn't   be   able   to   make   it.

5

Maggie set the table for five, and Lyra had the meal almost done, when there was a soft knock at the front door. Cinnamon raced ahead of Patricia and waited expectantly, already aware of who it was.

"Please come in," Patricia greeted their guest, who looked around the open-plan living area as she petted the beagle.

Raylene handed Patricia a bottle of white wine. "You have a lovely home. Thank you so much for inviting me."

Lyra could have pointed out that it was her house, but that seemed churlish when the farmhouse was originally built by her parents, so she smiled. "You're welcome. We know how hard it is to start over in a new place, don't we, Mom?"

Patricia nodded. "LA was a terrible culture shock after living here all my life prior to that."

"Then we have a lot in common, and I have to say that everyone is incredibly kind, and I love working at the diner." Raylene glanced at Lyra and smiled.

"I'm so glad. Make yourself comfortable, and we'll have a glass of wine while we wait for Dan." Patricia turned to the counter where the glasses sat. "Is white all right for you?"

"Yes, please." Raylene put her bag on the sofa, but joined Maggie, Lyra, and Patricia at the counter which separated the kitchen from the dining room. "It must have been hard to leave your family home."

Patricia smiled. "It was, but more important that I be near my daughter."

Raylene took the glass of wine from her. "And then you sold it when Lyra's career took off?"

Lyra tried not to flinch at the question. Keeping her life private and not opening herself up to people who wanted the gossip on a celebrity chef was the main reason for this, and she'd surprised herself by inviting an almost stranger for dinner. Since Rob McKenna's death, Raylene was their first guest. She took a deep breath. Why she left LA wasn't really a secret. At least not all of it. Patricia obviously agreed.

"Yes. In hindsight it was a bad move to sell." Patricia gave a short laugh. "Then again, you never know how things will turn out, and with all the decorating and modifications, this place is better than new."

"I have no decorating ability, whatsoever." Raylene shrugged. "I guess you have to see the end result in your mind or at least know what works together."

"I can't take much credit for this or the diner," Lyra explained. "Maggie has the vision and know-how to make it happen. She has a degree in design."

"A degree? Goodness, and you work for Lyra at the diner?" Instantly a pretty pink ran across her cheeks. "Sorry, I didn't mean that to insinuate it wasn't a good enough job, and of course you do a lot more than serve people."

Maggie waved away the apology. "I get that all the time when people hear of my degree, which I don't tend to shout about. In fact, it's funny because since moving to Fairview, I've used my creative skills more than any time over the last few years. Along with designing the house interior and doing the accounts, I work the layout and photographs for Lyra's cookbooks and liaise with anyone who wants her time. As for working in the diner? It's a great way to get some exercise and catch up with people."

"Wow, that's a mixture. Is being around people why you often work on your laptop at the diner?"

"To me, the whole cafe sound is soothing." Maggie chuckled. "Plus, I don't feel as though I'm missing out on what's happening in town."

"What about designing in general? Where do you get the ideas from, and how do you start a project?"

The questions suddenly reminded Lyra of the paparazzi who were always looking for a scoop. Raylene was friendly enough, and clearly enjoying herself, but now Lyra had that tightness in her throat from making sure she didn't say anything that could be taken out of context. It was silly when the questions weren't for her, and she turned to the oven to check on the food.

Maggie, who loved her job, was in full flight. "Online, books, and television. There are more shows than I can possibly watch about home renovations and restaurants. Knowing the colors you like and how you want to live is a big part of it." She snorted. "Although, Lyra's favorite color is red, so…"

Lyra narrowed her eyes. "All right, you've made your point, and the food is ready."

Maggie raised an eyebrow at the censure, then nodded. They had an ability to get their message across without words. Sharing unnecessary information with a relative stranger was a no-no, which Maggie had forgotten.

Just then Maggie's phone beeped, and she checked her messages. A cloud stole over her features. "Dan has an urgent job and wants a rain check."

Lyra shrugged. "No problem. That's the problem with owning your own business. Maybe you could take him a plate later?"

"Maybe."

Everyone heard the annoyance in her voice and stared.

Maggie forced a smile. "Of course, I will. Only he should have given a bit more notice after your hard work in the kitchen."

Lyra squeezed her shoulder. "It's truly fine. He would have struggled with all the female company anyway."

Maggie laughed. "You're right. Dan would be out of his depth for sure."

The matter resolved, they crossed to the table.

"This looks fantastic." Raylene sounded astonished.

"Do you mean the table setting or the food?" Maggie asked tongue-in-cheek.

Patricia laughed and placed wine on the table. "Don't answer her. She knows how clever her settings are."

"I meant everything, naturally," Raylene said, her eyes sparkling and looking less nervous.

"Well said." Maggie winked. "Now can we eat? I'm ravenous."

Lyra showed Raylene to a chair next to hers, which was closest to the kitchen, the place all hosts preferred to be. "Please help yourself before Maggie eats the lot."

Cinnamon forced herself under Lyra's seat, her eyes focused on their guest. A new person in the mix was always treated to a little wariness, even those that made a fuss of the beagle.

Raylene took a slice of lasagna, layered with meat, béchamel sauce, pasta, spinach, and slices of pumpkin. "This is so pretty; you must have made it."

A firm believer that people ate with their eyes first, Lyra nodded. "I did, and Mom made the garlic bread."

"Notice she left out that I made the salad," Maggie pouted.

"You're all so talented, and it seems that you have a lot of fun." Raylene shook her head in wonder. "I would have thought that living and working together might be difficult."

"It's absolutely awful." Maggie wrinkled her nose. "We're usually at each other hammer and tongs."

"Stop it, Mags," Lyra warned. "Raylene won't know when you're teasing yet."

"Oh, I'm deadly serious."

Patricia shook her head. "Pay her no mind. Maggie's a bit silly these days because a certain garage owner is courting her."

"Courting? Is that still a thing?" Maggie asked, cheeks bright pink.

Patricia tutted. "It is when two people are all gooey-eyed every time the other's near."

Lyra put up her hands. "Okay, truce."

"Mmmm." Raylene stopped laughing to take another bite and closed her eyes for a moment. "This is wonderful."

"Thank you—from all of us," Lyra said pointedly. "Are you enjoying working at the diner?"

"I love it. Everyone is so friendly, and I'm amazed that the customers are such wonderful tippers."

This surprised Lyra. Recently Vanessa mentioned that tips were down. "You must be doing a good job then. In fact, we've all been saying that we're so glad to have you onboard." Suddenly she had a horrible thought. Vanessa had never been invited to dinner. It was likely that she would feel slighted if she found out—and if was never an option in Fairview. Word got around town faster than a cold. Luckily, Vanessa was also working at the diner until closing, which meant she wouldn't have been able to come. Lyra would still need to explain the oversight as soon as possible, but there was nothing to be done about it tonight.

"How's the house you rented?" Patricia asked conversationally. "I hear it's nearby."

Raylene nodded. "It's at the end of the park walkway. The place is very small, but adequate for one person, and with all the trees, it's almost like I'm in the country."

Maggie chuckled. "You're certainly not far from it in any direction. I hear you come from LA too?"

Raylene moved her salad around her plate. "A suburb about forty minutes out of the city."

"That's handy." Patricia smiled. "We lived there for a couple of years. There's a lot going on all the time in a city like that. Do you miss home?"

"Not really."

A person's past wasn't always bake sales and roses, and the closed look on Raylene's face was enough to deter Lyra from asking more about her family or her hometown. "Do you have any hobbies?"

"Hobbies? I've never really had the time, but I do like to walk. Of course, I don't do that much after a day in the diner." She cut short her laugh, reddening. "Not that I'm complaining."

"We understand." Patricia handed around the garlic bread with an appreciative sniff. "A shift in the diner is a long walk on its own without adding any extra steps."

Raylene smiled. "I went down to the park on my day off. It is lovely around the stream. Very peaceful."

"Lyra goes there most days, before the children get out of school. Don't you, dear?" Patricia bit into a piece of bread and closed her eyes.

"The quiet and beauty is nice after the hubbub of the diner, and Cinnamon gets to forage. She loves the smells like any beagle would." A whack underneath her meant that the beagle heard her name, and Lyra grinned. "FYI. We don't mention W-A-L-K unless we're actually going for one."

Raylene laughed. "I'll bear that in mind. She's sweet and so well behaved. The customers adore her."

"They do, but it was touch and go at first. Some didn't think it right to have a dog on the premises, and a few were worried about her." Lyra snorted at the idea. "Once they got over Cin being on the veranda every day and appreciated that she never steps foot in the diner or kitchen, they started seeking her out."

"I can't imagine why they'd be scared of her. She seems to have a fantastic temperament."

Maggie chuckled. "Unless a person tangles with Lyra, she never so much as growls. Which is just as well because it's not pretty when she does. She's also got an amazing sense of smell and is the best guard dog ever, aren't you, girl?"

Raylene's eyes widened as the large tail whacked the closest chairs and legs, and she pushed her chair back a little, which made Lyra wonder if the woman might be a little scared of Cinnamon and didn't want to show it.

The woman frowned. "I have tried to stop people from feeding her."

"Good for you; we know how difficult it can be." Patricia chuckled. "She's a bit of a glutton, and given the chance, she'd eat anything."

Over dessert, which was a medley of fruit and homemade strawberry ice cream, the conversation moved back to the diner and how it was before Lyra purchased it, until Raylene smothered a yawn. She glanced at clock in the sitting room. "Gosh, I didn't realize how late it is. Can I help with the dishes?"

"We're all good, thanks. It won't take the three of us long." Much to her embarrassment, a yawn escaped Lyra too. "I'm sorry to admit that it gets to this time of night and I'm hopeless."

"In that case, I'll head off. Thank you so much for the meal. It was wonderful." Raylene stood and rubbed her stomach. "The walk will hopefully work off the amount I ate."

Cinnamon scrambled out of the too small space, almost upending the chair, and raced to the door.

"Oops!" Raylene grimaced at mentioning the dreaded word but didn't show any fear at Cinnamon's nearness. "I forgot about that."

"No problem. Cinnamon knows that it's too late for a stroll, but she's ever hopeful." Lyra grinned. "It's not like she doesn't have the full run of the place, and of the town, if she wants exercise."

"Aren't you scared she'll get lost if she wanders by herself?" Raylene asked as she collected her bag.

"No, much like Maggie, Cin's stomach is actually a clock, and she's always back in time for her meals."

Maggie shrugged good-naturedly, and they all laughed as the beagle studied them hopefully.

"Well, it's been a pleasure. Goodnight, everyone, and see you in the morning."

Lyra watched over the hedge until Raylene disappeared down the walkway by the diner before she closed the door. Luckily, Fairview was a safe place to live, and walking home alone late at night wasn't   an   issue.

6

Things were a little awkward in the diner once Vanessa arrived the next morning. It didn't take long to find out that her terseness was due to her exclusion from the dinner, and Lyra wanted to kick herself.

When Vanessa picked up a large order to deliver, Leroy sidled up to Lyra at the oven. "I'm sorry, but I mentioned the dinner with Raylene to Vanessa after you'd gone for the day. I didn't know it was a secret, and now she's fuming."

Lyra placed a tray of banana muffins in the oven and patted his arm. "It wasn't a secret. Just a silly oversight by asking only Raylene. I should have figured it would be an issue. Tell me, were you and Earl upset about not being invited either?"

His cheeks pinked up. "Don't take it the wrong way when I say that we're not bothered at all. Although, it isn't good that poor Raylene is bearing the brunt of her highness's jealousy."

"I see." Lyra tapped her chin. "Let me handle it when we're not so busy and I can get Vanessa alone."

"Good luck with that." He winked and went back to the grill.

For the rest of the morning, Vanessa seemed to be avoiding Lyra and Raylene was doing the same to Vanessa. It was childish, but sometimes it paid to let people work out their issues, and since the work was getting done and since no one was yelling, that's what Lyra decided to do.

On her walk that afternoon, Cinnamon was restive. She bounded along the path and kept coming back to Lyra and whining. "If only you could talk."

Cinnamon barked and nudged her in the back of the knees.

Lyra laughed. "I apologize. You want to show me something?"

The beagle grabbed her trouser leg and tugged her down to the water's edge. "Okay, you can let go now." From here she could see across the stream to the farmhouse, slightly hidden behind trees.

Cinnamon stretched up and tugged at her sleeve, and Lyra crouched. From this angle she could see into the kitchen. "Are you telling me that someone has been watching us?"

Cinnamon panted, which looked an awful lot like she was smiling.

"Who was it?"

The beagle ran up the slight incline and along the path, stopping several feet along it to check if Lyra was coming. Who wouldn't follow a beagle with a nose for trouble? Lyra mused. Anyone could be out walking and stop by the stream. If they walked around the bend, they'd look up to her back veranda, and if they carried on, they'd see the backyards of other houses. They reached the end of the path which led into a cul-de-sac. Two-story attached apartments lined both sides of the street.

Cinnamon sat and looked to her left and right, rubbing her nose with a paw.

"Did you lose the scent?"

The beagle woofed and sat dejectedly, gazing around them.

"Never mind. Whoever it was probably had an innocent reason for being there, like a tourist, and now they're long gone."

Cinnamon gave her a withering glance and slouched back the way they'd come.

Lyra clicked her tongue. Between temperamental staff and now her dog, life was frustrating. Her fingers itched. Baking something different was just what she needed.

Determined to put this incident out of her mind, she nonetheless had a chill race up her spine as they passed the place Cinnamon had taken her to. While she might have a vivid imagination, beagles worked on smell and probability. This did not help.

Positive thoughts were what this required, and plenty of them. Maybe if she gave Kaden a ring, they could have a good laugh over her paranoia. Although, to be fair it was Cinnamon's paranoia, and the beagle was rarely wrong.

Lyra arrived back at the diner, better for the walk and determined to share the story of her nosey beagle. As it turned out, Kaden was away at a conference for a couple of days and was unavailable, so Lyra settled into her baking with gusto. Once she was in the zone, it would take a full-scale war for her to notice any grumblings.

Maybe she would talk to Maggie about it.

But that didn't happen, because Maggie almost pounced on her the minute she got back, dragged her into the office, and closed the door.

"You won't believe who called?" Leaving no space for guessing, Maggie bounced on her heels. "Raine Riley! She wants you to cater for an animal-charity gala dinner she's organizing. It's two months away, but the only time she has free before she flies to New York is lunchtime tomorrow. She's happy to meet you wherever you like—in Portland."

The famous fashionista was an icon for the curvier woman, and Lyra adored her. "Wow. That's short notice, and I'm not interested in getting back on that roller coaster."

Maggie's eyes bugged. "Please tell me you're kidding. This would be great for your brand and might help you get back your shows."

A Lesson with Lyra had helped make her career, and the show was canceled after controversial stories about her were leaked to the press. "I'm done with that part of my life. I don't want to travel all the time or interview people who don't really care about food." She blanched, instantly regretting her snappy reply.

Her assistant's face clouded. "Sorry, I got overexcited. I know you're over all that, but I also know how much you admire Raine."

"No, I'm the one who should be sorry." It was true that she didn't want to step back into her old life, but Raine seemed genuine, and like Lyra, loved to help animal charities. Of course, she wanted to catch up with her and support the cause. The rest didn't have to follow. Plus, how could she disappoint Maggie? "It would be a shame not to hear what she has to say."

The loud gasp was just the tip of Maggie's delight. "Are you sure? Don't do it for my sake. You won't regret it. Just lunch, okay?"

49

"Just lunch," Lyra agreed, pleased that at least one of her staff was in a good mood. "Now what the heck can I wear that would be suitable? And where would we eat?"

Maggie waved away all her fears. "You have plenty of lovely clothes from doing the talk shows. I'll book you in at Phoenix even though Kaden's away. The staff will be attentive, and Raine will love the food."

As usual she made perfect sense. "I'll leave it with you, Mags, and since we're getting things done, I should find the time to speak to Vanessa."

"The staff would appreciate it. Let me get her for you."

Maggie shot out of the room and was back in less than a minute with Vanessa. Just as fast, she left, closing the door once more.

"Please take a seat."

Vanessa eyed her warily. "We're very busy."

"I won't keep you long."

The woman sat on the edge of the chair, hands folded over her apron.

"You don't seem to be yourself at the moment."

"Don't I?"

"No. And maybe that's my fault. I want to apologize for inviting Raylene to dinner last night and not including you or the others."

Vanessa sniffed. "It's nothing to do with me who you invite into your home."

"Maybe not, but it wasn't meant as a slight. It was a quick decision based on an observation that Raylene had no friends in town and might be lonely."

"A lot of people are lonely."

"That's true. As I say it was an oversight, and I wish I had invited you too."

"I'm not lonely, and even if I was, I certainly wouldn't expect dinner at my boss's house. It's not done, is it?"

"I don't know about other bosses, but I can't see the harm in an occasional meal together. We've done it before."

"We ate here at the diner," Vanessa pointed out forcefully. "You've always kept to yourself before now."

"Well, yes. You know something of my past. In the early days, it seemed best."

"Hmm."

Disbelief was evident in the set of her jaw, and Lyra was at a loss to make Vanessa see sense. "I can't change what happened, but please don't take out my mistake on Raylene."

"Is that what she's saying? That I'm a horrible person?"

Lyra's fingers gripped the arms of her chair. "No, she hasn't mentioned anything of the kind, but it's clear to see that you're not happy with her."

Vanessa glared. "I knew you'd take her side."

Sighing, Lyra placed her hands flat on the desk to relieve the tension. "This is not about sides. I would like you to all work as a team regardless of whether you like each other or not. And I'll tell Raylene and the others the same thing."

"Is that all?"

Unhappy with how this was ending, Lyra nodded, and Vanessa went back to work with a rod up her spine and likely taking nothing from their talk. Lyra followed her out and called Raylene into the office.

"What can I do to fix this issue with Vanessa?"

"We'll sort it out. She won't admit to being envious even though I told her she shouldn't be."

"That's what I told her. I suggest you give her some space and let me know if nothing improves."

With Raylene's nodded agreement and damage control a failure from her point of view, Lyra chose to spend the afternoon working on menu ideas for the charity.   Just   in   case.

7

Following a wonderful few hours with Raine Riley yesterday, Lyra was still enthused for the charity project. They'd covered a lot, but there was so much more to do to make it happen, and she looked forward to seeing more of Raine in the future to ensure it.

From Phoenix, where she'd caught up with Kaden's staff, she went straight home to the farmhouse to work on a menu that she'd suggested, and which needed tweaking. When Maggie got home that afternoon, Lyra was disappointed to hear that things were as bad as ever between Vanessa and Raylene.

It had taken all the joy from her day, but if she were honest, she hadn't expected an instant change, simply hoped for at least an effort.

By midmorning, Lyra knew she couldn't pussyfoot around the issue any longer. Maggie was set for mutiny, and Patricia was making excuses to get out of the kitchen as soon as Vanessa arrived. Leroy muttered at the grill, and Earl stayed away from everyone.

Raylene also kept her head down and worked almost feverishly, making it clear that she intended to keep out of Vanessa's hair, which was in an obvious tangle. So, how would Lyra tackle this? They weren't children, despite the behavior, and she needed both of them—not the headache they were creating. Vanessa was the main culprit, with pointed looks and ignoring

Raylene when she could, but experience told her there were always two sides to a story. What if Raylene was doing or saying something that no one had picked up on? She had to get out of here and think of a way to fix this before she had to let one of them go.

It was earlier than usual, but she desperately needed the fresh air to clear her head and called out to the staff who were nearby. "I'm taking Cinnamon for her walk. Please let Vanessa know."

"Should I take my break too?" Raylene's tone was hopeful. "We're pretty quiet right now."

"I'd prefer you waited until I get back in case Vanessa gets slammed."

Raylene nodded dejectedly. The darkness under her eyes had never gone and was even more pronounced today. Whether she'd had a bad night, or this was all due to Vanessa's attitude, it was clear that Raylene needed a break sooner rather than later.

In the process of removing her apron, Lyra had a change of heart. "Actually, you go ahead."

"Pardon?"

"I said you can go now. I can wait a little longer."

"If you're sure? Thank you." Yanking off her apron, Raylene raced out the door and didn't look back.

"With every hour, the tension around here is becoming unbearable," Leroy growled and slapped a burger pattie on the grill.

From behind her, Earl made the distinct sound of agreement.

Lyra nodded. "I know. Call me a coward about not tackling the elephant in the room before now. The problem is that I don't want to lose either of them."

Leroy raised an eyebrow and flipped pancakes onto a stack with steady and slick momentum. "Do you really think it might come to that over one dinner?"

"I guess it sounds dramatic, but you can never tell how people will react to a bit of censure. Anyway, I'll talk to them after lunch."

"Thank goodness," he huffed. "I don't care to endure much more of the frosty attitude when I didn't do a darn thing to earn it."

Lyra understood completely, having been grunted at once or twice by the usually eloquent Vanessa. "I don't think anyone is immune today."

"Definitely not me," Earl added, his head almost swallowed by the large pot he was scrubbing.

Knowing it had to smart that Vanessa had never been invited to the farmhouse while a newcomer had, Lyra was hoping that a little time to mull it over would help Vanessa get over the perceived slight. Since that wasn't looking likely, Lyra must find a way to get her back to the willing and pleasant server Lyra hired. Her gut told her that a simple apology wouldn't be enough. Not when Vanessa had developed a complex of not being good enough and after becoming a social pariah brought on by her daughter's fall from grace. She would likely view the oversight as a confirmation that this was still true.

"You'll find the answers out in the fresh air more than you will in here." Maggie pushed her toward the door. "I'll cover for Raylene."

Lyra smiled gratefully. "I will fix this," she threw over her shoulder. With a quick wave at the others, she went out to the veranda and down the back steps to the walkway. Cinnamon trotted beside her, glancing up every time Lyra sighed.

Taking a few deep breaths, she shrugged her shoulders several times to loosen the knot there. "You know, having staff can be a balancing act. I imagine it's like having a big family where people get offended at the drop of a hat."

Cinnamon chuffed.

"Yeah, I know. I should have thought how Vanessa would take the non-invite. Why didn't I think it through like I usually do?" They crossed the small bridge and turned left at the path heading toward the stream. "Leroy and Earl really don't seem to care about not being invited though, do they?"

Cinnamon tilted her head, caramel-colored eyes sparkling as if she were laughing at Lyra.

"You're right, they would have wondered why they were excluded too. I guess they're just better at hiding it. Well, I can't blame anyone but myself for this pickle."

The sound of voices halted her midstride, and her cheeks burned. Did they hear her talking to Cinnamon? Although, she did it so frequently, it was only a matter of time before this quirk was discovered. Perhaps if anyone asked, she would keep her conviction to herself that Cinnamon answered in her own way.

The conversation around the bend continued in whispered earnest, and Lyra recognized one of the voices. She couldn't make out the words, but fear dripped from the protestations.

Walking slowly around the tree that hid her, she spied Raylene at the edge of the stream accompanied by a well-dressed man who wore a hat. They stood side-on, and she saw Raylene's chin drop low as she listened to his reply. The gesture was one of defeat—the kind she'd seen when a contestant bombed out of the cooking competitions she used to judge. The man put a hand on her shoulder, and even from here Lyra saw her flinch. He snatched it away and made a menacing sound.

Lyra hurried toward them, and he glared at her. Muttering something, he hurriedly left in the opposite direction. Only then did Raylene turn to face them, clearly struggling to get her emotions under control. Cinnamon danced around her legs, which Raylene didn't acknowledge.

"Are you okay?"

"Yes, it's such a lovely day for a walk. I hope I'm not late." Raylene glanced at her watch and frowned. "No, I'm not. Did you follow me?"

Lyra frowned at the accusation. "You know I always come down here, and Maggie offered to cover for me. When I saw that man grab you, I was worried."

"Oh, sorry." Raylene rubbed a hand across her face. "I'm a bit discombobulated. That was no one I want to talk to. Salesmen are the pits, but I think he finally got the message, so no need to worry we'll see him again."

Fast blinking and several gulps indicated that Raylene wasn't being entirely truthful. Naturally it would be embarrassing to be caught out in a lover's tiff or some such argument. Even as she thought that, Lyra's instincts screamed there was more to it. She forced a smile. "I'm glad you're okay, but sorry you didn't get the break you needed."

"Me too." Raylene spoke flatly, glancing over her shoulder while stroking the beagle's head for a moment.

"Listen, I'm sorry for the way Vanessa's been acting. I should have asked her to dinner, and I'll speak to her about it when I get back. Is there anything else that the two of you are arguing about?"

"No! I mean, there's nothing, and I'd rather you didn't say anything yet. I can handle Vanessa, and I'm sure she'll get over it soon."

Surprised by the vehemence, Lyra stood firm. "While it would be nice if you two could handle this, it's already affected everyone on the team, so I don't feel I can let it continue."

Raylene's mouth opened a couple of times, but in the end she reluctantly nodded. "You've known Vanessa a lot longer than me, so you'll know the best approach to take. Well, I must go. I'll see you back at work."

Raylene still didn't look happy, but Lyra's mind was made up. Although it didn't need to be tackled this instant. "You don't have to hurry. There's plenty of time left on your break."

"Actually, I have something to pick up in town." With that, Raylene hurried up the path the way Lyra had come.

Confused at the dismissal, Lyra wondered if the woman simply didn't appreciate any intervention, or was she worried that Raylene would be worse to work with because of it. It was difficult to please everybody.

"She's working out all right, then?" Arabelle Filmore leaned over a gate at the back of her property which bordered the park.

Startled and yet a little puzzled that Cinnamon hadn't heard Arabelle come down her path, Lyra and the beagle made their way across the grass and up the small incline to the gate. "She seems to be a good fit. The customers like her, and she does have experience, which is showing."

"Is that right? Vanessa is a bit tight-lipped about her."

Lyra ignored the tinge of disbelief Arabelle conveyed in her question. "So Carrie-Anne informed me."

"Pssh! Carrie-Ann just wants the lowdown on whether the two of them can work together for longer than a week."

Lyra's skin prickled, and she knew she wasn't going to like the answer to her next question. "What does that mean?"

"Your new employee, or should I say your most recent, asks a lot of questions, and that's got Vanessa's back up."

The fact that other people felt as Lyra did was interesting. Perhaps Raylene had done something to annoy Vanessa unrelated to the dinner, which made more sense as to why the animosity had escalated. "Why are you telling me this?"

"Because Vanessa has enough to deal with. The town hasn't forgotten about Poppy residing in prison, nor what she did to get herself an extended stay there."

59

"I understand that, but I also thought things had calmed down and people had stopped commenting to Vanessa about her daughter's situation."

"That's because you keep those rose-tinted glasses on all the time."

Arabelle believed she could say what she wanted as bluntly as possible, and initially Lyra had no time for her, until she saw another side of the small woman. When Vanessa needed a friend after Poppy was sentenced, Arabelle had been there for her without reservation.

Of course, she hadn't changed completely, because Arabelle's heart was likely still in tatters. When the late Rob McKenna jilted her many years ago because of his son's dislike of her, Arabelle withdrew from him as well as everyone else. It could be put down to that alone, but Lyra imagined that Arabelle's caustic manner was mainly over the embarrassment that the town knew about the affair and subsequent split in detail. Whatever the cause of her sharp tongue, if anyone could empathize with Vanessa, it was indeed Arabelle.

"I'm still here," Arabelle reminded her impatiently.

Lyra shook her head to focus on the real issue. "Maybe I do try to see things positively, but what do you mean about Raylene and Vanessa not getting on, and why hasn't Vanessa mentioned this to me?"

"People don't generally complain to you, do they?" Arabelle scoffed.

"Really? You never have an issue with it."

Arabelle's mouth twitched. "That's because you being famous has never been a factor for me to treat you better or worse than anyone else. Others aren't so enlightened."

"Now you're being ridiculous."

"Not accepting the truth when you hear it is what's ridiculous."

Lyra tilted her head as Arabelle reached across to scratch Cinnamon's ear. The beagle leaned closer. "Okay. I'll investigate it. How are you?"

Arabelle looked down her nose. "Perfectly fine."

It was clear that this poking into each other's business was a one-way street, but Lyra didn't shy away from the glare. "You and Vanessa are back to being good friends then?"

Arabelle sniffed. "We're getting there."

"I'm not sure I ever thanked you for persuading me to give her the job."

Two dots of pink shaded Arabelle's smooth cheeks. "It's good to give people a second chance."

Lyra bit back a laugh. Vanessa was indeed lucky to be deemed worthy, as it was doubtful that Arabelle had considered anyone else in the town this way. "And even better when they take it and do their best. You can never tell if that will happen."

"I knew she'd do her best," Arabelle insisted. "Vanessa's never been afraid of hard work, but her husband was a stickler that the little woman stayed at home, raise the family, and keep house."

"You didn't like him?"

"I liked him fine." Arabelle shrugged. "He was simply old-fashioned. When he passed away, Vanessa was at sixes and sevens. He'd managed the finances, and suddenly she had to. She got bored and lonely and found the internet. Away she went, spending as if there were no tomorrow."

"I guess that put pressure on Poppy."

"Indeed. The poor girl was always sensitive, and she couldn't let on how her mom was out of control." Abruptly Arabelle stopped talking as if she'd said too much.

Lyra waited, and Arabelle sniffed again.

"Now, unlike some, I can't stand here gossiping all day. Just think on that newspaper article and who might have put it there." She gave Cinnamon one last scratch and headed up the gravel path to her back door.

Lyra crouched so that she was eye-level with the beagle. "Well, what do you make of that, Cin?"

The beagle licked her cheek, woofed, and raced away to the bushes further down the path, then came running back. She pranced about, and nudged Lyra to get her moving, then barked a couple of times.

"All right, calm down. I guess we do still have a bit of investigating to do," she muttered.

"Did I hear right?"

Still crouching, she turned too quick and fell sideways. Sheriff Walker stood behind her, which meant Cinnamon knew he was there, but Lyra was too intent on her thoughts to take heed. Red-faced, she ignored the hand he held toward her and scrambled to her feet. If he hadn't given her a fright, she might be happier to see him. "You're back already?"

His smile disappeared. "That sounds like you're disappointed and possibly annoyed."

"Merely surprised."

"Surprised, or worried that I heard you plotting? Would you care to enlighten me about your investigation?"

So, he had heard her. "It's nothing too bad. Apparently, my new employees have an issue with each other that I knew nothing about, which is causing a few headaches."

"That's not good. And you found out how?"

Lyra nodded at the house behind her. "Arabelle told me just now."

"Hmmm. She's usually right about things."

She chuckled.

"What? She may be grumpy, but she knows every resident, and therefore is a great resource if you need information about a person."

"Good grief. You use her that way?"

"Use?" He grimaced. "It's more of a matter of sharing information."

"I didn't think sheriffs did that with the public. You've certainly made it clear to me on more than one occasion that you don't like to."

"It's a matter of getting to know someone first, then deciding if you can trust them. That takes time, and it's not like you act on it, but it could help build a better picture of the problem."

Those gray eyes studied her intently, making Lyra wonder if he'd formed an opinion one way or the other about her. "Are you saying that you trust Arabelle, but not me?"

"There's trust to be had on so many different levels," he told her gruffly. "Anyway, I was headed to see Arabelle. Enjoy your... walk."

Cinnamon barked and ran around the two of them until, with a cheeky grin, the sheriff managed to get away. He'd done that deliberately. Saying walk in front of Cinnamon hyped her up, and he must know it by now. She'd bet two banana muffins on that!

8

Cinnamon raced along the stream and disappeared into the undergrowth of a thicket of trees, while Lyra fumed a little before admitting to herself that she was curious as to why the sheriff would be visiting Arabelle. And what information could they be sharing?

Excited barks meant the beagle had located a squirrel or another equally fascinating animal. What the beagle wanted was for the creature to run so she could give chase, and Lyra waited for whatever it was to be flushed out. Cinnamon wouldn't hurt it, but the poor thing would be traumatized and needing friendly intervention.

Whatever was in there wasn't in a hurry, and Lyra needed to get back to the diner. "Cinnamon! Let it be. Come on, girl," she called loudly to be heard above the barking, but the beagle barely hesitated before launching into another session.

Usually obedient, Lyra had no choice but to go see what interested her pooch so much that she'd ignore a command. Outside the thicket, a flattened patch of grass gave way to small broken twigs, and a patch of sun managing to get through the overhead branches shone on something. It must be a piece of metal, and if it was sharp, it could injure an animal. Crouching, Lyra duckwalked closer. The metal turned out to be the rim of glasses, and through them a man stared at her with a look of surprise.

What was he doing laying in here like that? "Hello. Sir? Are you okay?"

He didn't so much as blink. The sinking feeling in her stomach was horribly familiar. Pushing aside the remaining lower branches revealed that the man was bent in a funny angle—a knife stuck out from his chest!

Lyra recoiled, then forced herself to get closer to feel for a pulse. His skin was cool, and there was no sign of life. Scrambling back out of the bush, she looked around wildly. Where was her phone? Patting her pockets, she drew a blank, then pictured it on her desk back at the diner. In her hurry to get outside, she'd forgotten it, and now how would she contact the sheriff? Maybe he was still at Arabelle's. There was no choice but to go for help, and that was a good starting point. "Cinnamon, wait here."

The beagle crept toward the man, whined, then lay down beside him, resting her head on her front paws.

Feeling guilty for leaving Cinnamon this way, Lyra hugged her tight for a moment. "Good girl. I'll be as fast as I can."

Thank goodness for sensible shoes. Lyra pumped her arms and legs and made it to Arabelle's gate in a couple of minutes. Slamming through it, she ran up the path to pound on the back door.

It was opened by a very indignant Arabelle. "What is all this ruckus for?"

"I need the sheriff," Lyra gasped.

The man in question peered around door.

"Thank goodness you're still here. A man's been murdered in the park."

Walker slapped his hat onto his head. "Let's not jump to conclusions."

"I'd say no pulse and a knife in the chest makes things kind of obvious."

"Oh, my." Arabelle pulled the door shut behind them.

The sheriff put a hand up, which stopped her from coming any further. "Would you call the ambulance and let the station know?"

Pursing her lips, Arabelle nodded reluctantly.

"Show me where the victim is," he directed Lyra.

Running back the way she'd come, she was glad of the reassuring presence of the law, and they were soon with Cinnamon—and the deceased. The beagle came out of the thicket, her tail barely moving, a sure sign she was upset.

Walker crouched under the branches, the gap not really big enough for his bulk, and felt for a pulse. "He's gone. Did you touch anything?" he asked over his shoulder.

"Only his wrist and neck, the same as you."

Sirens wailed nearby, and Walker backed out carefully. "We need to preserve the scene as much as possible, and I'll take photos of him and of the surrounding area while we wait."

She nodded. "Just like when Leroy was attacked."

His thick eyebrows shot up. "Mmmm. At least we know it wasn't Poppy this time."

Lyra felt the blood leave her face and moved several feet away to slump onto the grass. Disbelief slipped away, and in its place was the memory of another murder. It was one thing to find a body and try to help, and quite another to know with absolute certainty that there was nothing to be done. Her hands shook, and she clasped them on her lap. Cinnamon slunk out from the bushes and put her head on Lyra's shoulder.

"Are you okay?"

Walker leaned over her, and she appreciated his closeness and the gentle tone in his voice. "It just brought the other murders back to me. I can't believe this is happening again."

He nodded. "It's natural to be shocked. I've seen a few murders, but it never gets any easier."

The admission from the staunch sheriff made Lyra feel a little better, as did the warmth of Cinnamon's paw on her leg. "It would be awful if a person got used to this sort of thing."

He nodded and tipped his head toward the man. "Do you recognize him?"

"No. How about you?"

"Never seen him before." Walker pulled gloves from his pocket. "I'm going to see if he has any identification then take the pictures. Will you be okay?"

Lyra pulled Cinnamon in to her side. "I'm fine. Did you notice how the ground is very flat around the entrance? He must have crawled or been dragged in there."

He raised an eyebrow. "I forgot that you have a good eye at crime scenes."

"Thanks. One of my lesser-known talents," she said wryly. "Why do you think he would crawl in there if he was already stabbed? I suppose he could have been hiding from the murderer."

Walker shook his head. "It would make more sense that he was dragged in."

"If that were the case, wouldn't there be smears of blood on the ground?"

"Hmm." He took out his phone and began taking pictures of the area, which was oddly smooth.

Lyra pulled a long blade of grass from beside her and shredded the thing while mulling over reasons why the dead man might be here. "I thought Fairview was a quiet little town. At least it was when I grew up here." She hadn't realized she'd spoken aloud until Walker answered.

"It usually is. We hadn't had a murder in years before…." His cheeks flushed.

"Were you going to say, 'before I got here'?" she croaked, her throat suddenly dry.

"I meant it as a time frame only. I'm not suggesting any of it is your fault."

"Right." She sniffed.

"Don't take it personally."

"That's easy to say when you don't have a business where people come by to gossip. If you think like that, then others will."

"Here's me thinking it was for the delicious food."

A siren sounded briefly, cutting off any form of retort if she'd had the energy to do so, and it wasn't long before Officer Moore and the ambulance team came over the rise. Sheriff Walker waved to them, and when they arrived, he explained the situation while the paramedic checked over the body.

"It's quite damp under here still, so time of death might be a little hard to gauge until I can do an autopsy. Best guess would be several hours," the paramedic explained.

Walker nodded. "Thanks. Let me know when you're done, and I'll swing by later. Janie, get his fingerprints and put them through the computer right away."

Officer Moore paled. "Y-y-yes, sir."

He frowned at her but didn't comment as they removed the body and placed it gently on the gurney.

Lyra felt sorry for the young officer. If this was her first murder scene, it was a doozy. She stood to get a better look at the man's face. He appeared to be middle-aged. It had been quite a while since he'd shaved, and a bruise covered the top of his face. His hair was short and fair, with dark roots showing here and there, as if he'd dyed it in a hurry or not known what he was doing. Dirt stuck to the legs of his trousers, and his fingernails were filthy. She gulped. Looks, as she knew, were often deceiving, but she imagined him as a drug dealer or a gang member. That would explain the knife. Or he could be an innocent person in the wrong place at the wrong time.

Walker took more photos and plucked a wallet from the victim's pocket. He dropped this into a plastic bag, then nodded to the paramedic who covered the body with a sheet. He took a couple steps closer to Lyra. "I'll see you back to the diner."

"I'm fine." She crossed the grass with him to the path.

"You don't look fine."

She took a deep breath. "By the time I get back to the diner, I will be. Besides, I have Cinnamon to keep me company."

"I think it's better if someone accompanies you."

The way he casually looked around them made Lyra nervous. The man was murdered, so the person responsible could still be around.

"Officer Moore, please escort Ms. St. Claire home, and I'll do the prints when I'm done here." Then he addressed Lyra. "I'll probably come by with some questions when I've dealt with some paperwork."

"Okay, but I can't think what I can add. We're just lucky that Cinnamon found him." She shivered at the thought of people walking through the park for days and weeks to come, not knowing a body lay nearby.

Walker bent to pat the beagle. "You are a remarkable dog, aren't you?"

Cinnamon rolled onto her back, loving the attention and praise, and her tail pounded the path beneath her.

"Sorry, girl. I've got work to do." He touched the brim of his hat and headed in the opposite direction.

Lyra watched him veer off the path and head back to the bush. He'd be checking all the surrounding area and then roping it off. Having seen all this before, Lyra turned away and picked up the pace. The sooner they left here, the better.

Since Janie didn't say a word and Lyra was lost in thought, it was a quiet walk back to the diner.

"Thanks for seeing me back, Janie."

Officer Moore simply nodded. Still pale, she seemed eager to get away.

Maggie was at the table in the kitchen and glanced up as soon as Lyra entered by the back door.

Then she was on her feet and at Lyra's side. "You look like you've seen a ghost. Are you okay?"

"Not really." Lyra slumped into the nearest chair. "Cinnamon found a body in the park."

The gasps that bounced around the kitchen meant everyone in the vicinity had heard.

Earl dropped a bowl of cutlery and scrambled on the floor to pick them up. "Sorry. I'll rewash them."

"I'm the one who should be sorry. It's a shock for all of us, but I should have told you with more tact, and since the police have it under control, please try not to stress about this."

"Do you know who it is?" Leroy called from the grill.

"No idea. I've never seen him before."

Maggie poured coffee and placed the cup in Lyra's cold hands.

Patricia tutted and squeezed her shoulder. "Unfortunately, bad things happen, dear. Let's not jump to any conclusions about this one."

"I haven't," Lyra assured her, not wishing to enlighten them as to how she knew it was murder.

"Maybe not yet, but that brain of yours will be working overtime."

Maggie made a humming sound of agreement.

Shifting uncomfortably at the truth of it, Lyra crossed her arms. "Tell me you're not wondering who he is and where he came from, Mom?"

"Anyone from a small town would consider it, but you'll already be onto how he died." Patricia said this matter-of-factly, then she saw Lyra's face. "Please don't say it was murder?"

"I guess you'll all know soon enough. It was murder, and you all need to take care. Other than that, I can't say any more about it."

There was stunned silence, then the door chime sounded several times in quick succession.

Maggie groaned. "Sounds like the knitting group is here."

Familiar voices could be heard, and by the level of excitement in them, they had obviously heard the news about the body. But did they know it was murder? From experience Lyra knew how a person died was usually kept from the public in case it messed up the investigation by giving up facts and clues that only the murderer would know. She'd ask the sheriff about it when he came by.

It was odd that, despite how he often annoyed her, she looked forward to seeing him—more than seemed reasonable given the circumstances.

9

Walker didn't come to the diner until later that day, when Lyra was in the kitchen keeping away from the sudden influx of customers. News traveled way too fast in Fairview, and she wasn't about to get stuck behind a mountain of questions and guesses about the dead man.

"Can we talk outside?" he asked quietly.

"Of course." She led him to the veranda, which was empty for a change. Cinnamon was rolling about on the grass but ran up the steps as soon as she heard voices and begged Walker for a pat. Apparently they were buddies now, which made her smile. "I'm glad you're here."

"Really?" His hand stalled over Cinnamon's stomach, and she nudged it so he'd continue. He gave her the side-eye. "Is that so you can pick my brains for any information I might have collected since I last saw you?"

His suspicious attitude might have made Lyra laugh if this wasn't important. "I haven't said anything about how the man in the park died—to anyone."

Walker raised an eyebrow. "And?"

"What I mean is, you didn't tell me I couldn't."

He shrugged. "I didn't think I needed to."

Oddly, this pleased her more than it should. "So, do you have any more details on the victim?"

"You think your silence needs a reward?" He sighed and glanced around the empty veranda while she gaped. "Don't answer that. We know who the victim is and where he comes from, but not why he's here. His name is Ardie Loxhay, and he's from LA."

She waited patiently, while Walker watched her closely.

"The name doesn't ring any bells?" he finally asked.

"Should it?"

"He's a reporter."

"Oh." Lyra couldn't help a small shudder. "I did meet a lot of them over the years, but that name doesn't mean anything to me. Should it?"

Walker reached into his pocket. "Maybe his picture will help jog your memory."

Confused, because she'd seen the man up close earlier that morning, Lyra took the photo he handed her and studied it. "He's not familiar."

"How about now?" Walker handed her a second photo.

This time the man had no glasses, dark hair, wore a suit, and was very much alive—and with those changes he was suddenly familiar. "Ace. That's what he called himself. Or at least, that's what everyone else called him. I'm pretty sure it wasn't a compliment. No wonder I didn't recognize him. He's dyed his hair since the last time I saw him, and he never wore glasses."

Walker handed her another photo. This time it was a side shot of Lyra being interviewed by a group of reporters after a competition. Ace held a microphone to her face—so close it made Lyra flinch as it had back then. Her cold fingers touched her lips at the memory of him aggressively invading her space along with several others. She shuddered once more.

"I guess you did have a problem with him in the past?"

"To be honest, I didn't like him, but he wasn't the only one. Some of the paparazzi are almost feral in the way they get a story at any cost, and they don't care if you're upset or not. I daresay it sells more copy if the subject is a sobbing mess."

"Maybe so." He shrugged his broad shoulders again. "The way he's looking at you is unnerving."

"Tell me about it." Lyra couldn't help a small smirk. "I developed a little trick of looking at their foreheads and imagining a big spider sitting there. That way I was always looking at a camera but not into their eyes."

"I can understand why. The red-eye from the camera matches his sneer."

"You're right." She grimaced. "He looks positively evil. By the way, you haven't asked me if I killed him."

Walker frowned. "Now why would you mention that?"

She rolled her eyes. "I know how this works. The person who finds a body is always the first suspect, right?"

That forced a snort from him. "It is Homicide 101."

"I bet it is, but I truly am shocked the body is Ace's and that I knew him. Of course, I didn't know his real name, or where he lived. I also couldn't say with any certainty which paper he worked for then, or if he does now."

"I assumed as much, yet none of that takes you off the suspect list."

Lyra thought about that for a moment. He said it without rancor, which was reassuring enough to let it go. "There had to be a reason for Ace to be in Fairview, and if I'm the only connection to him and have no idea why he's here, how will you work out the motive? Do you have any leads that aren't to do with me? Has anyone asked after him?"

"Give me a break. We just found the body. I've got a ton of work to do before we get to that stage. And it could be too early for someone to realize he's missing."

"Right." She nodded thoughtfully. "Plus, you need to ascertain his whereabouts in and around town to figure out who he's been in contact with. And then there's the knife and possible fingerprints."

He snorted again. "Are you sure you don't want to change jobs?"

Lyra glanced through the window into the kitchen. The place was humming, and even with a touch of antagonism now and again, she couldn't imagine being anywhere else. "I'm happy being a chef, thank you."

"Please remember you said that." The corner of his mouth twitched. "In fact, maybe I should get it in writing."

"Whatever do you mean, Sheriff?" She rocked on her heels and looked down.

"Drop the innocent act. I feel like I'm on repeat, but I must reiterate that I need you to stay out of the proceedings."

She blinked and crossed her fingers behind her back. "I wouldn't dream of getting involved."

"Hmmm." A wariness stole over his features. "I think I've mentioned before that I don't trust you."

"You have, and I'm still offended." She sniffed, though he had every right to feel that way. "I wish you'd appreciate that I don't actively seek out clues. Well, not as often as you obviously presume I do. And I only act on the ones that fall at my feet."

He rolled his eyes. "I can see this conversation is falling on deaf ears."

"Not at all. I understand you don't want me dirtying the waters of the case. Believe me, I would hate to do that. All I'm saying is that if Ace is here because of me, then someone else is either protecting me from him or there is more than one and they're much worse than your usual paparazzo. If you were at the center of a crime, wouldn't you have a few questions?"

He rubbed his face with his palm. "We have no idea if his being here *is* anything to do with you. He could have family members or friends in Fairview that he's argued with, or it could be a random act of violence."

"This is true." No matter that she heard the sense in what he said, Lyra simply didn't believe this was either a coincidence or random act of anything.

Walker sighed again. "Lyra, I need to get back to questioning people and do some digging. Meanwhile, if you think of anything, will you come to me and not go off on your own?"

The frustration in his voice touched her more so because he wasn't angry. They'd come a long way since she first came to Fairview, and he'd been anti pretty much anything to do with her. She didn't want to take a step backward by annoying him any more than she already had, and it was kind of sweet that he was worried about her. "Okay."

He blinked a couple of times. "That was a little too easy."

"I can't seem to win with you." She gave a wry smile. "You better go before I change my mind."

His mouth twitched again. "I'm beginning to wonder who is really in charge here," he muttered as he scratched Cinnamon one last time.

The beagle gave a soft woof, and they watched him hurry down the steps and into the walkway at the back of the shops.

"Maybe it is a storm in a teacup, Cin. I sure hope so."

"Are you talking to yourself again?" Maggie asked from the doorway.

"I never talk to myself. Don't roll your eyes. Maybe the odd time, but usually I'm talking to Cin. She's a wise beagle, aren't you, girl?"

Cinnamon made a chuffing sound and danced on her back legs.

"I can't deny it," Maggie admitted. "Now what do you know and what did the sheriff want?"

"Just between us…"

"And me."

Lyra whirled around. "Mom, stop sneaking up on me."

"Spoken like a guilty person!" Patricia tutted.

"I'm not guilty of anything except doing what the Sheriff told me to do—keep out of the investigation."

Patricia put a hand to her heart. "And you're actually going to listen to him this time?"

"I don't go out of my way to ignore everything he says," Lyra protested.

"That's an interesting use of words, dear. The sheriff is good-looking and a catch around these parts. I suppose you'll have to behave if you stand a chance of keeping on his good side."

Lyra groaned. "Stop that. You've got that matchmaking twinkle in your eye again, and I don't appreciate it."

"You're single and he's single." Patricia shrugged. "Dating isn't off the table, is it?"

"I'm not ruling it out in the future, just not with him. Plus, I'm busy and in no hurry to complicate my life. There's plenty of stuff happening right now that is far more important."

"Hmmm," her assistant mused. "What about Kaden, then?"

Lyra gave Maggie a frosty glance. "You know that we're just good friends."

"I bet it could be more if you wanted it to be."

"And ruin our friendship all over again? We've been through this, and there's no way."

"There is the saying that a good relationship should start with friendship," Maggie pressed.

"Like you and Dan?"

"Nice try, chef. Dan and I are doing okay for now."

"Oh, I'd say you're more than okay, dear." Patricia smirked. "I wouldn't be surprised if you were engaged by Christmas."

"What? No way. We're taking things real slow."

"Of course, you are. Only, do be careful not to let him get away. There are plenty of women in and around town who have their eye on him now that the truth is out that he doesn't have a wife and children."

Maggie gaped. The story she'd leaked about Dan had kept him free from other interest, but with it exposed as merely gossip, that would surely change, and Maggie didn't look so happy at the prospect.

With the spotlight moved, Lyra couldn't resist a dig. "How does it feel to be mom-pecked?"

"You're so sneaky. You turned this all around so you wouldn't have to talk about dating." Suddenly, Maggie's eyes narrowed. "Wait a minute, this is really a ploy not to discuss the murder, isn't it?"

Leroy poked his head out the door. "I hate to break this up, but Vanessa's swamped in the diner."

Lyra hurried inside, grateful for the excuse to leave those two to their own brand of madness.

10

"Where's Raylene?" Lyra asked Vanessa when she went by the counter with a tray of dirty plates.

It had taken Lyra a while to notice that they were down a server, and with orders piling up, it was now obvious that they were short-staffed.

"She called to say that she wasn't feeling well," Vanessa huffed.

"But she was in earlier, and she looked fine when I saw her at the park." It suddenly occurred to Lyra that this wasn't entirely true. There had been the guy she saw Raylene arguing with. Feeling queasy, Lyra got a mental picture of the actual distance of where the couple had stood and where she found the body. Was it a hundred feet? Two hundred? Maybe somewhere in between.

"What can I say?" Vanessa huffed, oblivious to Lyra's realization. "She refused to return from her break even after I told her she was needed, and it was hardly fair to leave us in the lurch at such short notice."

With that she plonked the tray down and grabbed a full one, disappearing into the diner before Lyra could react.

Was Raylene somehow connected to the death? She was definitely not herself when Lyra saw her in the park, and who was that man who grabbed her? Lyra finished with a customer as soon as she could, then followed Vanessa, who was collecting an order from Leroy at the grill. "Vanessa, why didn't you tell me about Raylene as soon as I got back?"

"I was busy, but I told your mom. I figured she'd tell you."

The belligerent look was a throwback and not a good reminder of how Vanessa had treated Lyra and many others not so long ago. She wasn't about to accept the attitude but did take onboard that the chain of command wasn't as clear as it should be. "We'll discuss that later. What I want to know is, did you two have an argument over it?"

Vanessa didn't look up from her tray and hurried past. "This food will get cold if I don't take it out."

Shocked at being dismissed this way, Lyra turned to Leroy. "Do you know any more about what went down between them?"

He shook his head sorrowfully. "I try to keep an ear out without butting in, but you know those two have something going on since the dinner business, and I think it just got a whole lot worse. To be honest, after Vanessa licked into her about getting back to work, I expected Raylene to return any minute."

Frustrated, she nodded at his honesty, then made her way across the kitchen. "Earl? Did you hear Vanessa and Raylene arguing today?"

Gulping, the young man did not meet her gaze and scrubbed a pot harder than it warranted.

"It's okay, Earl, if you don't want to tell me. I'd just like to get this sorted out before it escalates any further."

He looked up hopefully, glancing at the door to the diner before telling her quietly, "It was mainly about the dinner. Vanessa was upset over that, and she wondered if Raylene had done it on purpose."

"Done what on purpose?"

He hung his head. "Got you to invite only her."

"I see." Lyra was already sure everything hinged on this rather awkward mistake. "How did you feel about not being invited?"

"Oh, I don't mind." His smile was brief. "My mom says I don't have the right table manners for company, and I wouldn't like to offend anyone."

Lyra clutched her stomach as if hit by a mule. "Oh, Earl. That has nothing to do with it. The truth is, I felt sorry that Raylene was new in town and lonely. I simply didn't think it through."

"We get it," Leroy said soothingly. "Vanessa is unfortunately a different matter. She saw it as a slight, and I guess she's borne a few of them lately."

He must be referring to Poppy. Some people had been quite cruel and said outright that a mom had to take responsibility for the actions of their child. Darn it, she'd really messed up. "Don't you worry, Earl. I promise I'll get this sorted."

He gave her a hopeful smile and went back his scrubbing.

Making a call to the station, Lyra felt guilty, but as much as she didn't want Raylene to be involved in murder, the incident in the park was too important not to share. Officer Moore explained that the sheriff was busy and would call her when he could.

With that taken care of to the best of her ability, Lyra went out to the counter, watching to see how Vanessa treated the customers, and was gratified that the woman's anger was confined to the kitchen.

She had to wait until the late afternoon before another opportunity to speak privately with her server eventuated. The woman did a good job of avoiding her, bustling about and sweet-talking the knitting group into buying meals to take home to keep busy. Meanwhile, Lyra spoke to Patricia, who was enjoying the afternoon off and had no idea things had escalated. After asking Earl to watch out for customers while he cleaned down tables, she had Maggie be on standby. Only then did she call Vanessa to the office.

At first she thought Vanessa would refuse, but Lyra held the door and waited until she entered, and pointed to a seat. "While I don't want to turn this into more than it is, I have to say that I'm disappointed. You've been working here long enough to know I wouldn't be happy with your handling of the situation. You should come to me if you have any issues with Raylene, which clearly you do."

Vanessa pursed her lips and glared at Leroy through the doorway. Fortunately, he was busy cleaning the grill. Or pretending to be.

"She doesn't like being told what to do and ignores me when I set her straight," she huffed. "The very next day she started showing off about going to your place for dinner and rubbing my nose in me not being invited." Vanessa gave an impatient toss of her head. "Not that I expected one."

It was clear that she was more than bothered by it and wasn't getting over their issues anytime soon, but the business about Raylene taunting her was hard to accept when she seemed to want to please Vanessa. All Lyra could do was try to minimize things without seeming to negate the hurt feelings. "I told the others, and I'm sorry that I didn't make things clear to you before now. I invited Raylene because she was new in town, and that's all it was—a spur-of-the-moment decision."

Vanessa sniffed. "It's none of my concern."

Hitting her head against the desk wasn't going to help, yet the urge to do so was very strong. "It is if it upsets you, then it concerns us all. I want this to be a happy place to work, and right now, it's not. Walking on eggshells is not a nice way to spend the day, and no one wants to work in an environment like that, including me. Everything has been pleasant until the dinner, am I right?"

Vanessa shrugged. "Mostly. Like I said, Raylene doesn't like being told what to do, even though she asks a ton of questions and I have to repeat myself constantly."

"Maybe asking instead of telling would have better results. Isn't that the way you'd feel about it?" Lyra said this gently, hoping her words would sink in. "Some people need longer to register what is said. You're a fast learner, but what if Raylene's fear of getting it wrong again is messing with her?"

Vanessa smoothed her apron for a few seconds. "You think that's why Raylene didn't come back to work? She was scared to face me because I may have been a bit harsh?"

It didn't escape Lyra's notice that Vanessa seemed to have forgotten that she'd accused Raylene of rubbing her nose in the invite. She'd already decided it was an exaggeration if not a figment of Vanessa's mind, but she could see that the tide had turned, so there was no point in harping back to the conversation.

"That could be it, or maybe she is genuinely ill. Let's wait and see if she's back at work tomorrow. Although, the last thing we need is a sick person serving in the diner, so we need to be sure that she's okay and doesn't feel forced to return. Having another pair of hands makes all our jobs easier, so let's hope she isn't thinking of leaving."

The blood drained from Vanessa's cheeks. "If she doesn't come back and it's my fault, you won't sack me, will you?"

Lyra chewed her bottom lip for a moment. "I'll do my best to not have that happen, and if you keep in mind what I've said, your job is safe. Maybe I haven't told you recently, but I think you're a great asset to the diner. We all do."

"Apart from this," Vanessa said through quivering lips.

It was as good a time as any to clear the air. "You know, I ran a restaurant and had a lot more staff than this to organize. I had a head chef under me and someone to take care of the restaurant, but it was still my business. The diner is on a much smaller scale, so we don't need a formal hierarchy. When I'm not around, Mom is in charge, and if neither of us are here, then Leroy can fend any questions, but basically you're all responsible for your tasks. Everyone needs to work in harmony, help each other out, and lead by example every time we get new staff. Last, if anyone needs a talking to, I'll be the one to deal with it."

Vanessa's cheeks returned to pink, but she nodded. "I'm sorry I overstepped."

The fact that she sounded so sincere gave Lyra hope that they could work this out. "Thank you. Your apology means a great deal. I'm sure we can get this sorted once we all sit down, talk this through, and clear the air. Don't you think?"

Vanessa brightened slightly. "I hope you're right. We got on well before all this."

Lyra smiled encouragingly while her fingers crossed involuntarily at her sides. Imagine if she'd gone to all this trouble to have the women reconcile only to find out that her faith in Raylene was misguided.

11

When Raylene arrived at work on time the next morning, she came straight to the office where Lyra was anxiously waiting. "I'm so sorry about yesterday," she blurted. Though even darker under the eyes, she didn't look sick, merely tired, which was a relief.

"What happened?" Lyra asked. "I heard you were ill."

"I almost fainted and was light-headed. It came on so suddenly, and I didn't think you'd want me back like that. I did call and tried to explain to Vanessa."

"Yes, she told me. Well, I'm glad you feel better. Are you sure you didn't have a bug? We can't have you working today if you did."

"I feel 100 percent, but I understand what you mean. There was no vomiting or anything like that. When I thought about it much later, I think it was due to lack of food, and that I didn't drink enough. It does get very hot in the kitchen even with the fans on."

Lyra suspected it was more a case of the argument being key to how Raylene was feeling. All that stress could make a person ill. "It is very important to drink plenty and eat regularly to keep up your strength. If you're sure you're okay and you had no other symptoms…"

"I swear, I didn't," Raylene said earnestly.

"Okay. But if that changes, please let me know right away."

"I promise."

Raylene was about to rise when Lyra forestalled her. "Before you start work, we need to have a short meeting."

Raylene paled, obviously expecting the worst, and Lyra went to the door without further explanation.

"Maggie, can you look after the counter for a while?"

"No problem."

"And please ask Vanessa to come to my office."

Maggie crossed her eyes at Lyra. Sometimes being the boss positively sucked, and her friend empathized, but wisely didn't comment.

Raylene didn't say anything while they waited, and Lyra shuffled a couple of papers, preferring not to start the conversation until both servers were here. She sincerely hoped it wouldn't descend into anything ugly. After finding the body, and not being able to sleep because of that as well as this nonsense, she simply wasn't up to refereeing them.

Vanessa came to halt when she spied Raylene already in the office.

"Before either of you jump to conclusions, this is not an ambush. Vanessa, come in and shut the door, please." Lyra pointed to the other chair. "While I can't force you to be friends, I do need you to be adults about the animosity between you and how we can resolve, or at the very least, mitigate it."

"I'm sure we're fine…," Raylene began lamely.

Lyra put a hand up. "This won't work if we aren't all honest about what's going on between you two. Nobody in this kitchen has pointed the finger, but outsiders have commented, and the boys couldn't deny that something isn't right. I don't care what you do outside these walls—actually, I do, but it isn't my business. In here it's different because we all need to get along. Let's get this out in the open so we can move on."

Vanessa stared straight ahead while Raylene fussed with her skirt.

Lyra tapped her desk. "Someone needs to start."

"She thinks I pick on her." Vanessa motioned beside her.

Raylene gasped. "No, I don't."

"Then why do I have to repeat myself all the time? You're not deaf, are you?"

Raylene's eyes widened, then just as suddenly she crumpled in on herself, sobbing into her hands.

Vanessa tutted. "What did I say that's so bad?"

"Maybe you could tone it down a little," Lyra suggested as she handed Raylene a tissue and waited while the woman struggled to get herself under control. There was no mistaking Raylene's distress. The question was, why did she act so over the top to a throwaway comment?

Vanessa gulped and turned slightly toward her coworker. "I'm sorry, Raylene. I know I can be a bit sharp. I didn't appreciate how sensitive you are until now."

Lyra wanted to smile at the backhanded apology, yet it seemed to be working.

Raylene had straightened her back and blew her nose. "It's not your fault, Vanessa; it's mine. I didn't want to tell Lyra the truth because I had to have this job."

"I'm not following." Lyra frowned. "What have you been lying about?"

Flinching, Raylene wiped her face rather firmly. "I've been deaf in one ear for years and have issues with tinnitus in the other one. I do hear some things, and can lip-read well, but the diner gets so noisy, and in the kitchen with the mixers going all morning and the dishwasher… well it gets tricky to concentrate on one voice. I had hearing aids until recently, but they were broken." She gulped. "And I can't afford new ones right away."

Lyra gaped, and Vanessa wasn't much better.

"So, you couldn't always hear me?" Vanessa eventually asked loudly.

Raylene grimaced. "When people yell, the sound is distorted, and they get annoyed when you constantly ask them to repeat themselves, so I do rely heavily on lip-reading. The thing with that is you must be facing me, otherwise I don't have a clue unless I catch my name, or a person indicates what they want me to do."

"That explains so much about you misunderstanding what I ask you to do and all the repeating." Vanessa smiled wanly. "You poor thing. I wish you'd said something. I figured you were ignoring me and thought you were better than me."

Her mouth did that thing people did around deaf people to enunciate each word and her voice became slow and drawn out. Even Lyra grimaced.

"Sorry, Vanessa. I should have told everyone from the start and accepted the consequences. There's no way I would think I was better than you. I admire how hard you work and the professional way you deal with people. And, since we're being honest, I hate to mention it—thanks for trying to talk clearly—but that exaggerated way you're doing it just makes it worse."

Vanessa blushed. "I'll try to remember that. So, what do we do now?"

Lyra thought for a minute. "Raylene's told us what she needs. We must face her and talk slower, but not in a funny accent." She winked and was rewarded with chuckles. "Plus, we'll inquire about new hearing aids today."

Raylene blanched. "I honestly can't afford them just yet. Maybe in a month or so."

"You let me worry about that. They're necessary from a safety aspect, so we'll work something out that won't stress you, but will make all our lives easier."

"You can have my tips until they're paid for," Vanessa offered. "Not that I get as many as you."

The words held no animosity, and Raylene smiled. "I don't know what to say. I felt sure I was going to get fired, and here you are being so nice." She sniffed. "Thank you, Vanessa. Meanwhile, I'll try harder to get things right, so you don't have to repeat yourself. I can imagine how annoying it is."

Vanessa patted her arm. "We'll muddle through until the hearing aids arrive."

"And we're all good about the dinner issue, which was totally my fault?" Lyra dropped that into the mix and watched their reactions closely.

Vanessa stiffened ever so slightly. "Absolutely. Who you have in your home is nothing to do with me, and it was childish to react that way."

So, things weren't quite back to normal, but Lyra had another brain wave, which she hoped would be better than her last. "I'm glad you feel that way, because the whole team is invited for dinner on Sunday night. We'll close early and enjoy an evening together where none of you have to cook or do dishes."

"You don't have to invite me," Vanessa insisted.

"I'm inviting the whole team, the way I should have done in the first place. The diner couldn't function as well as it does without everyone doing their part. Now, let's hear no more about it so we can get back to work."

The women thanked her again and scurried back to the diner.

Maggie stepped inside and took one of the seats. "Judging by the big smiles, that must have gone well."

"Better than I hoped. Did you know Raylene is almost deaf?"

Her assistant's eyes bugged. "What? How can that be?"

"She lip-reads. Until I can get her hearing aids fixed, we need to make sure we face her when we're talking to her."

"The poor thing. It must be hard to understand when she's taking orders."

"She's obviously used to reading lips while typing on a tablet. I don't think I could do both things at once."

"Me either."

Lyra grinned. "By the way, we're having a dinner party at the house on Sunday night. Can you give me a hand with setting it up?"

Maggie's face lit up. "A dinner party sounds great. Who's invited?"

"Just the staff, including Dan."

"We'll need another table and more chairs. I'll get Dan to bring some over from here on Saturday afternoon."

Lyra leaned back in her chair, satisfied that she'd handled the situation well enough. "I knew I could count on you."

"As long as I don't have to cook, we're a great team."

"We are indeed." Lyra laughed. "You know, I think I might invite Kaden."

"That's a good idea. You haven't seen him in weeks."

"I know, and I did try to get him to come to dinner the other night, but he couldn't make it. There's so much to tell him, and with Sunday usually a quiet night in the restaurant, he should be available."

Maggie nodded, her eyes fixed on a space above Lyra's head, in the way she did when making mental notes. "Anyone else?"

"I don't think so."

"Not the sheriff?" Maggie asked innocently.

"Why would I invite Walker to a team function?"

"I don't know. You two seem to be getting on better these days. Besides, Kaden's hardly part of our team either."

"Hmm. If I didn't know better, I'd think you've been hatching something with my mom. That road does not end well, my friend."

Maggie gave a slight bow. "Duly noted—my friend."

12

A day later, Maggie did a repeat performance with the same paper that had previously given several digs at Lyra's reasons for leaving "fame and fortune."

"It seems our local diner is having problems again. With another murder on the doorstep which could affect sales, our ex-famous chef must be thinking that another change of town is in the cards. Is this another case of bad management, or is our diner owner more than she appears?

And what of the staff? Nothing has been heard of Poppy Fife, who is still doing time for the murder of local man Robert McKenna, yet her mother has conveniently taken her place behind the counter. Isn't that a little too close for comfort for Fairview residents?"

It went on in the same vein, but this time didn't mention her by name, and the picture was of the diner before the revamp. That was bad enough, but mentioning Poppy and insinuating that Vanessa might be guilty of something made Lyra's blood boil.

She banged her desk with a fist. "This is out of order, and I've had enough. Turning the other cheek isn't an option here."

Maggie clicked her tongue. "Uh-oh. I don't like that look in your eyes."

"Let's hope it's enough to get the editor off my back."

"Want me to come with you?"

"No, I think one-on-one will be sufficient, and there's no time like the present."

"Go get 'em, tiger."

Lyra folded the paper and tucked it under her arm, then marched out through the veranda exit, where Cinnamon joined her on the mission. She nodded at several people sitting at tables enjoying the fresh air, determined not to engage. One or two gave a surprised look at her behavior, but she was in no mood for small talk. While she hadn't exactly shared her life story since coming here, she had been reasonably accessible to everyone—except the press. Maybe that was her mistake? If she'd kept the local paper happy with snippets, they might have left her alone. It was too late to change that, but somehow she had to fix this. When Vanessa read that article, it would cut her to the core.

The office for the *Fairview Gazette* was on Main Street. Lyra took the alley and joined Main at the next intersection. Two doors down, she hesitated at the door where a logo on the window beside it announced: "Honesty with Honor."

"Really?" she muttered and pushed open the door. "Wait here, Cin. Hopefully this won't take too long."

A young woman with curly blonde hair sat at a small reception desk, eyes wide and mouth slack. Clearly, she knew who Lyra was and probably why she was here.

"Good morning. It's Trista, right?"

"Y-yes."

"Could I see your editor please?"

A quick glance at a partition told Lyra that the person in question was behind it.

"I'm afraid Mr. Eckhart is busy this morning. I can take your number and get him to call you when he's free."

"This is extremely important, so I'll wait until he is available." There were two chairs to her left, and Lyra sat in the one facing the partition.

Flustered, the young woman stood uncertainly. "He might be a while."

Lyra raised her voice. "I have all day if necessary."

"I'll get you some water." Trista hurried through the gap.

A terse and muted exchange followed with one very deep voice. It seemed that Mr. Eckhart was not only in, but unhappy about his visitor.

Several minutes dragged by, and neither Trista nor the water appeared. Having made the decision to force his hand, Lyra was on her feet when a short man with thick glasses resting on his forehead stepped through the opening.

He coughed and came across the room. "Ms. St. Claire. How nice to see you."

"I wish I could say the same, Mr. Eckhart."

His hand, in the process of lifting to shake hers, flopped to his side. "I see. You've come about the article?"

"Articles," she emphasized, waving the paper in her hand. "What I want to know is why all of a sudden you're printing this stuff."

He didn't meet her gaze. "People are interested in you. It's not the first article I've written about the diner," he said defensively.

"That is true in the broadest sense, but I've lived here for several months now, and you haven't printed anything like this before. Have I done something to offend you?"

"Not at all," he said plaintively. "I've heard nothing but good things about you and your diner."

"Then I'm at a loss as to why you'd try to hurt not only me but my staff by writing nasty conjecture."

He paled and spoke as if by rote. "Unfortunately, news of any kind is what sells papers."

Something was off here. He made it sound as if he hadn't wanted to print the articles, which made no sense. Unless he didn't have a choice. "Do you own this paper?"

His chin jutted. "I'm the editor, and I run it."

His sudden defensiveness was alarming. "That's not the same thing, is it?"

His Adam's apple lifted several times. "I can't divulge who owns the paper."

Warning bells that kept her awake in the past screamed inside her head. "I appreciate that you may have been asked not to, but I will find out."

He took a step closer and lowered his voice. "If I may offer a word of advice, Ms. St. Claire? You'd be wise to let this alone."

His earnestness took away any perceived threat words like that would ordinarily convey, and she hesitated a fraction. "That isn't possible, Mr. Eckhart—not when my family and friends are being attacked. Good day, sir."

Her stomach twisted as she walked back to the diner. Cinnamon, who'd waited patiently for her outside the door, rubbed against her leg and nosed her hand. Her fingers found the soft head, and she paused to let the tension ease a little, comforted by having the beagle near. "At least we know we're not imagining things. Someone doesn't like us. More precisely, someone doesn't like me."

The caramel eyes glistened sadly, and Lyra nodded. "I don't understand it either, and I can't let this go." With the diner in good hands, she carried on back along Main Street and crossed over before she got to it. From the other side of the road, she could see inside, and her heart warmed a little at the sight of customers and staff going about their day. Had Vanessa seen the paper yet?

Some might think that Fairview was a boring small town, and yet it was so far away from being that right now she could weep. Lifting her head, she continued to the police station, more determined than ever to get answers.

Janie Moore offered a commiserating smile as Lyra entered. "How are you coping after that horrible business?"

"Are you referring to the article?" Lyra said a little tersely.

Innocent eyes stared back. "What article? I meant finding the body."

Lyra grimaced. It wasn't as if she'd forgotten, but the story had scratched an exposed nerve and put the murder to one side, which wasn't right. "Yes, that was certainly upsetting for all of us. Is Sheriff Walker in?"

"I'm afraid he's out right now with the other deputies." Janie gave her a speculative glance. "Can I help with anything?"

"Do you know who owns the *Fairview Gazette*?"

Janie nodded effusively. "Lester Eckhart's owned it for years."

"According to him, he doesn't any longer."

Janie blinked disbelievingly. "That's news to me and probably most of the town. He bought it about a decade ago. I was just a teenager, but I remember there was a big send-off to the retiring editor."

"Hmmm. It sounds like the selling of the paper this time was a closely kept secret."

"Secret? In Fairview?" Janie scoffed.

Lyra smiled. Janie was a sweetie, and remembering her horror at having to touch the body, and not wanting to see the bad in people, perhaps she wasn't entirely suited to the dark side of police work. "I'm sure I can find out the information on line; I just thought the police would know."

"It is odd no one said anything to me. If I hear anything about that, I'll let you know." She sounded a little miffed.

Lyra thanked her and headed back to the diner and her laptop. There was a reason that Eckhart was printing this stuff about her, and the reason had to have a person behind it. A person who possibly had more on their mind than sullying her reputation, and wasn't afraid to kill.

She started with the facts she knew, writing them on a pad.

Ardie was a paparazzo.

The paparazzi had done a lot of damage to her career in the past.

Someone wanted to discredit Lyra.

The owner of the *Fairview Gazette* was until recently Lester Eckhart.

The new owner wanted to remain anonymous.

Next she googled Ardie. He had no articles lately. In fact, for some time. Before that he'd worked for a small tabloid. She called the number attached to it and asked for him, expecting the reply that he was no longer employed there, but also got added information that he hadn't been for several months. That time frame jarred. It couldn't be coincidence that it was around the same time she moved to Fairview.

After that there was nothing more on him.

Next she checked on Lester Eckhart. He'd been a reporter for thirty years, and while he'd done nothing major, he seemed to have a solid reputation. The previous owner had started up the paper and had only sold due to ill health. She could find nothing on the current owner.

That was odd. It was a small town, and someone must know. She could ask Karl Lowe, the local lawyer, who was honest and kind, but he might not be able to say anything because of client privilege.

That left her back where she started. The only one who could find out the truth was Sheriff Walker, but would he tell her if he did?

13

Technically Sunday was Lyra's day off. Today things were different. She could have opted for a BBQ or something simple but relished the idea of giving her staff the chance to experience a lavish meal as a thank-you for their hard work.

The AC blasted through the open-plan lounge, dining room, and kitchen while she cooked, in the zone. This was the place all chefs aspired to, and once there, things became automatic, but not in a robotic way. There was no need to think, only see, feel, and taste.

Immersed in her work for some time, she eventually became aware of someone else in the room when he moved.

"Kaden!"

The scramble of claws from the back veranda resulted in a blur of brown-and-white beagle launching herself at Kaden. "Darn, I didn't want to disturb you." He laughed and crouched to hug and scratch the wriggling dog.

"Don't be silly." She grinned, wiped her hands on her apron, and ran across the room to throw herself at him just as he stood.

Stumbling back a couple of paces, he managed to keep from falling. "Wow, great welcome!"

"I'm so glad you could make it," she mumbled into his shoulder.

"How could I miss a dinner party by the famous Lyra St. Claire?"

She pulled away and shook a finger at him. "There'll be none of that this evening. I want my staff to look at me as just a chef."

His eyebrow shot up. "Really? You are their boss, right?"

She blanched. "Okay, as their boss too. But a friendly, and nothing extraordinary, boss."

"You don't want much." He laughed again. "How about you fill me in on everything that led to this epiphany and generous gesture?"

Lyra batted her eyelashes. "Since you're early, maybe you could lend a hand while I do?"

Kaden snorted. "You mean I have to work on my day off?"

"If it's not beneath you."

"I guess I still owe you for helping me when I was short-staffed and again when I relaunched Phoenix."

"You don't owe me a thing. Having a fire in a restaurant is a nightmare for all restaurateurs. Helping you was exactly the right thing to do and what our friendship needed. Plus, I seem to recall you returned the favor." Their history spanned several years. Some of them turbulent. Their friendship had survived everything from murder, sabotage, bullying, and theft, stronger than ever. "Let's agree that helping each other is what we do and leave it at that."

"You're the boss." He gave a mock bow. "What can I do?"

She pointed to the large refrigerator. "You can be in charge of the fish dish."

"Suits me."

"We're having salmon, a duck main, and a surprise dessert."

"A surprise?" He laughed. "That's always interesting."

They worked side-by-side, with Lyra thankful that she'd spared nothing when designing this kitchen. It meant that there was more than enough room to avoid the two of them banging into each other, as well as plenty of work space to tackle their courses.

"Where's Patricia?"

"She's over at the diner working on the dessert—hence the surprise. I didn't want her to, but you know Mom. She can't help being involved if she thinks it will help me. Much like you." The smile became somewhat forced, and he saw it.

"What are you dying to tell me?"

She flinched at his choice of words. "How do you know I have something on my mind?"

"Are you kidding me? Your body is humming, and I've seen that anxious look way too many times for it to be a coincidence."

"Okay, but you have to put it in perspective and not go all overprotective on me."

He smirked. "After all this time, you should know that I am capable of that. Unless we're talking another murder."

Lyra dropped the salt container. It hit the counter and rolled to the edge, where Kaden reached out a large hand and caught if before it hit the floor.

Distracted, he juggled it for a moment "Another murder? I did not see that coming."

"Neither did I. Cinnamon found the body a couple of days ago in the park and led me to it."

"Are the police convinced it's murder?"

"Absolutely." Her nose screwed up. "It was gruesomely obvious."

"Hmm. In that case, let's leave out some of the details. Are you sure the city isn't a safer place to live?"

"It does make a person wonder," she admitted sadly.

They continued with the prep and the conversation.

"Please tell me that they caught the murderer."

"Not yet." She sighed. "The thing is they have no idea why he's dead or even why he was in Fairview. Except…"

"I don't like the sound of that, but go on."

"He's a paparazzo, and I kind of knew him."

He put down a very sharp knife. "Kind of—what does that mean?"

"I saw the guy hanging around my shows. He always bugged me for an interview. Or I should say that he pushed a large microphone in my face a few times and yelled questions at me."

"Sounds like a real nice guy. I bet the police find that interesting."

"There's more. When I saw him, I didn't know who he was until Walker showed me a picture taken of him a while back. It was almost as if he was in disguise."

"You're kidding?"

She explained about not recognizing him because of the dyed hair, mustache, and glasses. "I know people change their appearances all the time, but not guys like him, who desperately want to be known and then continually recognized as the one who got a scoop."

Kaden paused chopping herbs. "Then a disguise makes no sense if he was here to get an interview."

"Exactly. If I was the real reason he came to town, he certainly never contacted me, but I can't think of another reason for a man like him to be here, unless he had family, but the sheriff says no one's come forward to make inquiries about a missing person." She let out a long sigh. "None of it makes sense, but when I think of Ardie's being in league with the person who killed him, the whole thing becomes more sinister."

"But if they were working with Ardie to discredit you, why would they kill him?"

Dan and Maggie interrupted their contemplation by hefting a table up onto the front veranda. Kaden hurried to give them a hand, and the men brought it inside. Any more discussion would have to wait until after the dinner.

Kaden shook Dan's hand and gave Maggie a hug. "Good to see you both. How are things with the garage?"

Dan beamed. The garage had become his passion after being left it in a will by the late Rob McKenna, and he was rightly proud of it. "Great. People have been awesome about me being the new owner, and they're certainly keeping me busy. How's Phoenix?"

"Back to her old self, with full bookings most nights." Kaden matched that beam and raised it with a heartfelt sigh.

Maggie rolled her eyes. "Okay, boys. Before you get carried away talking about your babies, let's get the table in place, then you can go get the chairs, Dan."

"Your wish is my command," he mocked.

Maggie poked out her tongue, and Kaden flashed Lyra a grin as if to say this romance between the two of them was ticking along nicely. Which it was, and much nicer to contemplate than what they had been discussing.

Maggie went to work on the table settings, and soon the place looked very festive with candles along the middle surrounding a beautiful, handcrafted flower arrangement in the center.

"This is so clever, Mags," Lyra congratulated her.

"Thanks. I thought the wood might come in handy when I found it a few days ago down by the stream."

Once the chairs were put around the two end-to-end tables, everything was ready, and none too soon, as her guests began to arrive.

"Come right in." Lyra beckoned Leroy, and from behind him the others appeared. Everyone seemed shy, but none more so than Earl.

"Hey, Earl. Want to see some pictures of a hot rod that's currently in my garage? She's pretty sweet."

The young man's eyes widened. "Yes, please, sir."

"I'm just Dan. One of Lyra's workers, like you. Actually, you have more seniority, as I'm just a part-timer these days."

Leroy nodded his approval and handed Lyra a bottle of wine, while Patricia squeezed past everyone and took a covered pan to the kitchen. Her friends and family had lightened the load, and since she rarely had time off, she appreciated it more.

Vanessa gave her a posy of flowers. "These are from me and Raylene."

"You didn't have to bring anything," Lyra gently scolded them, knowing that the flowers must have come from Vanessa's garden and thinking how sweet it was that she had included Raylene in the gift.

"It may have been a long time between the last one, but one doesn't go to a party without a little something," Vanessa insisted.

"Well, thank you all. Rather than stand around, why don't you all take a seat, and I'll bring out some refreshments. Sit wherever you like."

"Let me do the drinks."

Dan handed Earl his phone to scroll through the pictures and took orders, which left Lyra free to bring out the salmon starter. Interestingly, Vanessa and Raylene sat together, as did Leroy and Earl opposite them. When the others took their seats, Maggie had a space next to her for Dan, and Lyra was next to Kaden. Mom sat on Leroy's other side, and the two of them smiled benevolently at the rest.

The sight of her team in one place and looking happy made Lyra's heart swell as she tapped her wine glass. "Welcome, everyone, to our first team dinner. Hopefully we'll have more, but we're very lucky to have an awesome chef, Kaden Hunter, and he has made the starter, which is his signature dish."

The others exclaimed at the pretty plates of salmon on a bed of eggplant, spices, and tomato.

"This is very fancy," Raylene murmured to Vanessa.

"I'm sure it's as delicious as it looks." Vanessa nodded. "You let me know if you need something repeated."

Lyra thought the night couldn't get any better than that.

14

Due to the warm night, the front door had been left wide open. A shadow flitted across it, drawing Lyra's attention, and a familiar face appeared.

She hurried across the room, hoping for news about the case. "Good evening, Sheriff Walker. Is everything okay?"

He wore jeans and a shirt, his face a picture of uncertainty as he took note of her guests. "I'm sorry, I had no idea you were having a party."

"It's a thank-you to my staff, rather than a party." For the second time in the last week, she seemed to have got her planning wrong, but she could change that. "I'm glad you stopped by. We have plenty of food. Why don't you join us? Unless this isn't a social visit?"

He eyed the group at the table, who were watching intently, his gaze settling on Kaden. "It was a mixture, but I won't intrude."

She put a hand on his arm and pulled him into the room. "Don't be silly. I insist. Dan, could you get another chair, please?"

Dan raced out the door, and Maggie moved all the places a little with the other's help. Mom rustled up another setting, and Kaden brought out more fish. It wasn't until Dan added the chair from the diner and they all sat again, that Lyra realized the room they'd made was on Lyra's other side. Now she was in the middle of Sheriff Walker and Kaden. Mom and Maggie looked very pleased with themselves.

"Go ahead before the food gets cold," Lyra told them.

They tucked into the wonderful dish with relish—except for Raylene. To Lyra it seemed she wasn't enjoying it at all. Of course, some people didn't like fish, and Lyra didn't want to make a fuss and embarrass her by asking.

"Lyra tells me you come from LA, Raylene. What do you think of Fairview?" Kaden asked.

The woman stiffened, but she managed a weak smile. "I like it a great deal."

"What about the diner? I'm sure it's a little different to ones in LA because of the chef, right?" Kaden grinned, but his attempt to draw her into conversation failed again.

"It's a good place to work, and the food is wonderful." She picked up her glass and turned away.

The next course was the duck with a medley of roasted sliced vegetables. Lyra had timed the cooking just right and was delighted to serve them the perfectly cooked meat with a spicy plum sauce and roast-vegetable medley.

Again, everyone ate enthusiastically, except Raylene. She kept glancing at the sheriff. Her throat twitched, and she drank so fast and often that Dan topped up her glass several times without any comment from her. Nerves aside, she hoped it wasn't the food that didn't appeal, and she avoided answering any questions about herself though most of them tried to engage her. She could see by the way he watched Raylene that Walker had also noticed.

"What made you stop by tonight, Sheriff?" Patricia asked casually.

This instantly dragged Lyra's attention away from Raylene.

Walker wiped his mouth carefully on a napkin. "It was a courtesy call to say that so far there is no news about the victim."

Patricia grimaced. "Well, let's not discuss that on such a lovely evening."

Everyone nodded, Raylene more enthusiastically than the others.

Lyra couldn't help herself. "Although, it is such a shame that this happened close by. I hope whoever killed him has left town."

Again, murmurs of agreement surrounded her.

Raylene took a hefty swig of her wine and kept her head down. "Do you think that's likely, Sheriff?" She slurred ever so slightly.

"Without knowing why he was killed, it is hard to say, but my deputies are keeping a close watch on Fairview, so there's no need to be scared."

"But we should take care just in case?" Lyra asked.

Walker frowned at her. "Naturally."

He would have said more, but Kaden interjected.

"From what she's said, Lyra seems to be the common denominator here, Sheriff. I would hope, if nothing else, that your office is keeping a close eye on her."

Walker stiffened. "The victim might know Lyra, but that doesn't mean the killer does. However, I can assure you that my staff are vigilant in watching over Fairview, so you needn't worry on that score."

Raylene scraped back her chair, looking around her wildly, and Maggie jumped up, taking her by the elbow.

"Let me show you where the restroom is."

"T-t-thank you," Raylene mumbled.

Patricia noisily cleared the plates, her eyes narrowed when she got to Lyra.

Okay, maybe she wasn't as circumspect as she thought in bringing the subject out in the open, but anyone could see that Raylene was nervous being around the sheriff, and Lyra, with that familiar tightening in her stomach, would bet a batch of savory muffins that there was more to it than just an aversion to the law. However, whether she was onto something or jumping to conclusions, in front of her coworkers and the sheriff wasn't the right time to question the woman.

Lyra followed Patricia to the kitchen and set out the dessert dishes.

"What are you doing, asking all those questions?" Patricia hissed.

"Nothing, Mom."

"Pinky swear."

Lyra glanced over the counter at the awkward group and plucked spoons from a drawer.

"Aha. I thought as much."

"Let's talk about it once they're gone, okay?"

"You just bet we will, young lady." Patricia huffed and lifted the cover off an apricot crumble. "Oh dear, I forgot to make the custard."

"That's okay. I have some more homemade ice cream in the freezer. I'm sure our guests won't mind."

Patricia's annoyance was likely due more to having to wait to find out what Lyra was thinking than the lack of custard, but she nodded and got out the ice cream to roll into balls while Lyra served the crumble.

"This looks delicious," Walker said enthusiastically.

"Mom made it," Lyra explained.

"Then the talent is genetic."

"What he said," Kaden added.

"I've never had this before," Earl told them. "I didn't know it was a thing until I went to school."

Kaden's eyes widened. "But you would have had some of Lyra's at the diner?"

"Not yet." Earl smiled shyly. "They look great, only I'm saving my money for a car."

Shocked at his admission, all thoughts of Raylene being guilty of something disappeared momentarily. "Earl, I told you when we opened that you could have whatever you wanted to eat."

Confused, he nodded at Lyra. "Oh, I do. I have a burger every day and fries."

"I can vouch for that," Leroy added.

"Surely you can have a dessert too?" Kaden asked.

The young man blinked. "That would be greedy."

"If that's the only reason, then I will be very annoyed if you don't have dessert every day from now on, young man." Patricia sniffed, and Leroy patted her shoulder.

Earl looked around at his coworkers and noticed their grins. "Okay? And thank you," he added.

"I don't know where you got the idea from, and in future, if you're not sure about something, ask any of us." Lyra nodded in satisfaction. "Now that's settled, does anyone want coffee or tea or something else?"

Maggie escorted Raylene back to her seat. "We'd love coffee," she said pointedly.

An hour later, most of the group were chattering like old friends when Vanessa made noises about the time and getting home. Kaden and Walker were slightly frosty toward each other as they insisted on clearing the table—together. Raylene was still slurring her words when she did speak. Still, as her staff left, and she had a moment to digest everything that had taken place, Lyra counted the night as a success.

Maggie and Dan went for a walk to work off the meal—so they said. At Patricia's insistence, Lyra left her to empty the dishwasher and went out to the back veranda where she'd noticed Walker and Kaden had slipped away to. They leaned on the railing, looking out across the water, talking quietly. She heard the word "danger," and then they noticed her and were silent.

Walker turned and made room for her, so she was once more in between them. It was a little awkward, and in her mind, she pictured her mom with a satisfied smirk. This was a game she had no intention of playing, especially when some of the contestants didn't understand the rules.

"Do you think Raylene knows something?" Kaden asked.

Surprised that he was asking her and not Walker, Lyra could only stare for a moment, then surmised they'd already had a conversation about it. "You are talking about the murder, right?" she clarified.

Kaden nodded. "She was very uncomfortable as soon as you came in, Sheriff."

"Call me Finn. I must be losing it if I didn't notice. Are you sure?"

Finn? Her gaze shot to him. Not knowing his first name until now was suddenly weird. Obviously, the sheriff had a first name, but Lyra had only ever thought of him as Walker or the sheriff. "I thought the same thing—about Raylene," she blurted. "I didn't think anyone else noticed."

Kaden laughed. "I guess being around you during those other cases has made me conscious of things like that. Or I took my cue from you. Who can say?"

"Who indeed," Walker muttered. "How about the two of you let me into whatever you think is going on with Raylene."

"She was fine until you arrived," Lyra pointed out. "She couldn't eat, which I put down to not liking the dish at first, but she barely touched anything else and was decidedly tipsy by the time she left."

"Personally, I think drunk would describe her better," Kaden said wryly.

"You're right," Lyra conceded. "Perhaps it was nerves about the dinner, but I'm picking it was all about you, ah, Finn." She tried the name, which seemed to suit him, then shook her head at how irrelevant that was right now. "Luckily, Vanessa offered to take Raylene home. It's not a long walk if they take the path by the stream. About. Somehow it slipped my mind, but I wonder if you know…"

As if on cue, a scream rang out across the water, and   Cinnamon   howled.

15

"Dan, please stay with Mom and Maggie," Lyra begged as she ran by the kitchen, thankful the couple had returned. Then she raced through the house to the front door with Cinnamon on her heels.

Walker and Kaden reached it ahead of her, having used the wraparound deck. The three of them ran across the lawn, through the hedge and down the walkway behind the shops to cross the small bridge before heading left down the same path the two women would have likely taken. A chill settled in Lyra's stomach, as it occurred to her what Cinnamon had found just off this very path a couple of days ago.

The beagle raced ahead and yipped in the distance. It was a relief to hear her make that sound instead of barking, which meant she was happy. Vanessa stood under a streetlamp, and as they got closer, they could see that she had her arms around Raylene, who sobbed into her shoulder. Many houses around the park had lights blazing, and there were faces at some windows. A scream like that would have disturbed all but the deepest sleeper.

"What the devil happened?" Walker growled, his hand reached for the hip devoid of a weapon and floundered there briefly. "Are you both all right?"

"Thank goodness you came." Vanessa spoke over Raylene's head. "She swears that she saw something between the trees and suddenly she was incoherent and shaking like a leaf. I don't know what to do with her."

Walker's eye narrowed as he looked around them. "Did you see anything?"

"Not a thing." Vanessa nodded to their left. "One minute we were talking about the lovely evening, and the next minute she was screaming and pointing."

Beyond the trees in the direction indicated, lay the stream. It hugged a slight bank on this side all the way down past Destiny to the large lake in Maple Falls. Had Raylene seen something or someone? Or had she remembered that the body was found not far from here and after a few drinks her imagination brought on a panic attack?

Walker, along with Kaden and Cinnamon, took a moment to check the area, but Lyra had the impression that this was for Raylene's benefit rather than the sheriff thinking anyone would be there. After all, with the noise, if someone was out there, they would surely have moved on in a hurry by now. "We should get Raylene home where she'll feel safer," Lyra said when they came back.

Walker put his hand out to Raylene, who shrank away from him. It was clear by the way she clutched Vanessa's blouse that she didn't want anyone else near her.

"It's okay, Raylene. The sheriff's just here to make sure we get home safely. Now, go ahead and put one foot in front of the other, and before you know it, we'll be there."

Lyra admired Vanessa's calmness in the face of Raylene's breakdown. Walker skirted around them to lead the way down the path to where it ended at the base of a small enclave of single-level homes. They were tiny and mostly one-bedroom rentals with no fences.

When they got to the third door, Vanessa handed Lyra Raylene's worn handbag. "The key will be inside."

Lyra hated to ferret among the woman's belongings, and it was dark on the doorstep. There was a light above them, but it was such low wattage that she could barely make out anything in the bag. Finally, she heard the tinkle of keys and pulled them out, tucking a few papers and an odd ball of plastic that came with them back inside. Unlocking the door, she found the switch for the lights, which revealed a sparsely furnished sitting-cum-dining room that was shabby, but clean.

Vanessa escorted Raylene to the two-seater couch, but Raylene had other ideas.

"I'd like to freshen up," she said shakily.

Vanessa walked her down a small hall then, but Raylene entered alone and shut the door behind her.

Walker checked the small bedroom, then peered out the windows, while Kaden stood helplessly by the door. When Walker came back, Lyra beckoned to both men and headed to the kitchenette. "I'll get Raylene a glass of water," she said to Vanessa, who was now sat on the couch, and the woman nodded blankly at no one in particular.

The three of them squeezed into the small area.

"What's up?" Walker asked suspiciously.

"I was about to tell you something earlier," she said quietly. "Something I should have mentioned before, only I thought Officer Moore would have told you."

"I don't like the sound of this."

She gulped. "The day Cinnamon found the body, Raylene had an argument with a man in the park."

Both men gawped at her.

"Why the heck am I hearing about this now?" Walker's voice shook with barely contained rage.

"I'm sorry. I forgot about it."

"How do you forget something like that when there's a murderer on the lose?"

"Calm down," Kaden interjected firmly. "Lyra will have an explanation if you care to listen."

Thankful for Kaden's intervention, she took a steadying breath, not wanting to get Janie into trouble, but since he never got the message, this was a big deal. "I told Officer Moore and thought you must have spoken with her about it and accepted what she said."

He grimaced. "Clearly I didn't; go on."

"Raylene told me the man was a salesman who'd been harassing her, and he was leaving town because he finally got the message she wasn't interested."

"What was he selling?"

"I didn't ask her."

Walker frowned. "Did you believe her?"

Lyra considered that. She had accepted Raylene's story and yet... "Not really. I wondered if he was an ex-boyfriend."

"You do know that ex-boyfriends can be murderers?" Kaden pointed out sardonically.

"Look, I'm not a police officer..."

Walker grunted. "Really? I'd never have guessed. What did he look like?"

It felt so long ago, but she concentrated and came up with a couple of things she could recall. "He was above average height, solidly built, and had dark hair."

A movement to her left made Lyra look down the hall, where Raylene stood at the open bathroom door, watching them.

Walker broke away first and indicated the couch. "Come and sit down."

Many emotions crossed the woman's face as she took a seat next to Vanessa, the most prevalent appeared to be fear. Sweat dotted her forehead and upper lip, and she rubbed her face with a shaking hand.

Lyra brought her a glass, and Raylene took several gulps of water. "Thank you all," she croaked. "I'm okay now and embarrassed by the fuss I've caused. I had the idea that someone was watching us, and it seemed so real at the time, but now I just feel silly." Straightening her back, she finger-combed her hair with a grimace. "I might have had a glass too many, and most likely it was the breeze blowing branches around and creating shadows that scared me. You should let these nice people take you home, Vanessa. That way I'll know you're safe."

From a quivering mess to being self-deprecating, the sudden change in Raylene's body language and her tone was huge. She might be a good enough actress for the men to accept she'd only had a moment of foolishness, but Lyra didn't believe it for a minute, and Vanessa didn't look convinced.

"Are you sure?" Vanessa frowned. "I don't mind staying all night if necessary."

Raylene gave her tight smile. "I'm a big girl, and a good night's sleep is all I need."

"I'll go only if you promise to lock the door and call if you change your mind."

"I will," Raylene promised, staggering to her feet. "I apologize again for ruining a wonderful evening."

"You've had a difficult few days, and it's easy to see things in shadows among the trees," Walker told her kindly on their way to the door.

The four of them waited until the lock clicked before heading back the way they came. A few steps down the path, and Walker stopped. "Go ahead; I need to make a call."

Lyra wanted to ask him why he hadn't made it at Raylene's, but he shook his head imperceptibly, so she went with the others, and when Lyra looked over her shoulder, he had disappeared. She hoped he would be safe out there with no gun.

Vanessa's house wasn't far from where the commotion had begun, and they traipsed up to her back door. The woman stepped inside with a sigh. "Normally, I'm not bothered by the dark, but I have to say that scream put such a fear into me that I'm glad to be in my own home."

"It was a horrible-sounding scream from back at the farmhouse, so it must have been horrendous to have it come from beside you," Lyra commiserated.

"I almost fainted myself," Vanessa admitted.

"I think we should look around to put your mind at rest so you can sleep. Would that be okay?"

Vanessa hesitated, before she nodded. "I guess knowing no one is in here would help."

The lights had been left on, and the place was homely and welcoming as the three of them traipsed around the three-bedroom cottage—Vanessa as close to them as she could get. It must be hard for this private woman to have strangers in her house, but these were exceptional circumstances.

Each room was immaculate, including Poppy's, which looked like the young woman would be back at any minute and not serving a sentence. A basket of knitting sat in one corner by a comfy chair in the sitting room, and on a small table beside this was a photo of her. There were many more dotted around the rooms, including one beside what must be Vanessa's bed. Poppy looked so happy in every one of them, belying the darkness she was suffering by losing her father and having her mom become so dependent on her financially. Lyra hoped the young woman would get well and be happy again one day.

"Thanks for seeing me home, and again for that wonderful meal."

"You're welcome. See you tomorrow."

They got back up to the road where Walker waited, a little breathless. "I've left a deputy to watch the house."

"That was fast," Kaden said appreciatively. "Raylene's behavior was strange, don't you think? One minute she was a mess and then she had herself under control."

Walker made a rude sound. "I wasn't happy about leaving things where they stood, so I went back to ask her about the man in the park. Raylene agreed she had too much wine and convinced herself she saw someone, but it wasn't that guy. And before you ask, I have no idea if she's telling the truth. About any of it. The man in the park could have been a salesman, which is odd in itself to conduct business like that. Either way, there's no proof he came back tonight. What does worry me is that the murderer is still out there, and this is a coincidence I can't ignore."

A large tree groaned beside the walkway, and Lyra shivered. "All I know is there was no way to fake that kind of fear, and I'm glad you have her house being watched."

"It's just for tonight. I got the man's name reluctantly from her, and I'll check him out when I get back to the station and file my report, so I'll leave you here."

"At this time of night?" Lyra asked with surprise.

"If I wait until the morning, I might forget something, and there's a chance I could unearth details about this salesman."

"Good night then." She turned away with Kaden, who said the same.

"And, Lyra, thanks for a lovely evening."

"Now who's exaggerating?" she said over her shoulder.

He chuckled as he headed up Main Street.

Kaden nudged her. "Well, that was a different way to end a dinner party."

"Never say I don't provide entertainment."

"I don't know how you do it."

"Find drama?"

"Well, yes." He snorted. "But you handle it so well."

"Gah! Don't tell me that murder is becoming my thing? That will hardly look good on my new billboard."

"A billboard? That is great news. You're finally going to put Fairview on the map."

She snorted back. "You've been hounding me long enough to do it."

"Which means you're ready for the world to know that Lyra St. Claire lives here."

"I was," she said ruefully. "When I thought the paparazzi were mostly out of my hair. I was even prepared to live with a little backlash. Maybe I should rethink things again. Do you think there's something more than imagination going on here?"

"Who can say? Although, I agree with Finn. It does seem too much of a coincidence that the dead guy was a reporter."

"Me too. Someone killed Ardie or Ace for a reason. I was thinking that it could be another paparazzo. They do bicker among themselves a great deal. Each wants the scoop or at least to be the first to publish a story, even if it's only by hours."

"You mean they want it so bad they might manufacture one like the articles in your local paper? Oh no, I'm beginning to sound like you!"

She laughed softly. "Sorry. I guess sniffing out clues is catching."

"Not for this chef. I'm happy with no mysteries hanging over my head."

"Hmmm, after what we've been through together, and the fact that you're still here, I could argue, but it's far too late tonight. You will stay, won't you?"

"I better if you have room. While I couldn't compare to your friend Raylene, I did have too much wine to drive back to Portland."

On the veranda of the farmhouse, Dan, Patricia, and Maggie waited impatiently.

"Thank goodness, you're all okay," Mom called out. "How are Raylene and Vanessa?"

"They're fine." Deliberately, Lyra downplayed what had happened. "Raylene had a panic attack over shadows in the woods."

"Too much alcohol?" Dan suggested.

"Probably." Lyra yawned. "I need some hot milk and my bed. But first let's find somewhere for Kaden to sleep."

"Don't go to any bother," Kaden said. "It's one night, and the couch is perfectly fine."

"No need," Dan interrupted. "When I heard you were coming to the dinner party, I assumed you might stay the night, and decided it was a timely nudge for me to shift my stuff to the apartment above my garage."

"What? You didn't tell me you were moving out," Lyra protested.

"Having your house back to normal is long overdue. There's only the painting to do to finish the apartment, and I can move a bed around for that. I've been buying furniture over the last month, and I'm sorted, so you can keep the bed here. You did buy it after all."

"Well, that's settled," said Maggie with a twinkle in her eye.

Clearly the two of them were in on the surprise of him moving out—and happy about it. As much as

Lyra would miss having Dan around, the couple needed their own space, and she had a feeling this was the catalyst for their future relationship. The only fly in the ointment was having Maggie move out. Maybe it wasn't going to happen just yet, but she'd bet a banana muffin that it eventually would.

This was such a weird evening in so many ways. Apparently, you could be delighted, sad, and scared, all at the same time.

16

In the morning Kaden had breakfast ready by the time Lyra was showered and dressed. Ceremoniously, he pulled a chair out for her at the table. "Morning. Patricia said she'd start your shift so we could eat together."

"While this is fantastic, you do know there's a diner right next door?"

"True, but I know once you get in there you won't sit down for hours. Selfishly, I wanted to have a last meal with you before I go."

She shuddered. "Don't say it that way."

He waggled his eyebrows. "Getting superstitious?"

"No, but we shouldn't put it out there in the universe."

"Wow, where is the Lyra St. Claire who doesn't believe in woo-woo things like that?"

"Are you kidding? My life over the last couple of years has been a roller coaster of bad stuff happening." She slid into a chair and chuckled. "Sorry, that was a little dramatic."

He crouched beside her and took her hand. "Are you having a breakdown?"

That made her snort. "Not yet, and a pity party is totally unnecessary. I love my life, and there were just as many good things that conspired to bring me here as the bad everyone seems bent on bringing up. I wish people hadn't died, but I don't regret living in Fairview—yet."

"The murder naturally has you rattled, and last night's escapade didn't help," he said reasonably. "And a couple of articles is not everyone."

"I know, but it's more than that. I don't want to be the cause of bringing tragedy to town. It bothers me a great deal that because of me it could happen."

"You can't stop troubles people from doing what they do, and those murders were not your fault."

She knew he spoke from his heart, and she desperately wanted to believe him. "Perhaps not, though I would like to understand why it keeps happening around me."

"It must be frustrating and upsetting. I wish I could help work it out, but I know you're in safe hands with Walker." He winked. "I mean Finn."

"He is a good sheriff."

"I have no doubt. And he thinks a lot of you."

Heat hit her cheeks. "Don't be silly."

Kaden rolled his eyes. "Can we not pretend anymore? He likes you and you like him. There, it's out in the open."

"Look, we've only recently become friends, and there's nothing more to it than that," she insisted.

"Hmmm." Kaden stood and poured her coffee, then uncovered a plate of bacon and scrambled eggs. "So, your relationship is similar to yours and mine?"

She shrugged. "I guess."

"Really?" He filled her plate and sat opposite her, then took a long swig of coffee. "Do you want to go on a date with me?"

The forkful of egg stalled on the way to her mouth. "Sure. We could do something together next week."

"I mean a real date. We could hold hands and kiss. You know, girlfriend, boyfriend stuff." He waggled his eyebrows suggestively.

Swallowing hard at the mouthful that decided to lodge in her throat, she drank some coffee and wiped her mouth on a napkin. "Kaden, what the heck are you talking about?"

"The truth is, I don't interest you in that way."

She shrugged again. "Well, no, because we're not that kind of friend."

"But the sheriff does because he is that kind. Am I right?"

"No. He... I... We..."

"Yes?"

"Oh, shut up."

"I do love you," he said around a mouthful of bacon.

"Then why are you such a pain?"

"Because you have your head in the sand and it's time to take it out, look around, and have some fun."

"I do have fun. With you, Maggie, and Dan."

"You love your job and all of us, but if you call chasing criminals and solving crimes fun, which I suspect in an odd way you do, then Sheriff Finn Walker is your man."

"Dating someone because of their job is plain crazy."

"Is it? There are a lot worse ways to choose a partner or a friend."

She tilted her head. Darned if he didn't make a lot of sense, but she wasn't about to let him know that and thereby encourage him on his one-man show to get her a boyfriend. Unless Mom and Maggie put him up to this? Also, he must like Walker a great deal because this was the first time he'd ever pushed her toward another man.

His phone dinged. Kaden checked it, smiled, put it back in his pants pocket, and went back to eating with a silly look on his face. *Interesting.*

They'd changed the subject and were chatting over coffee when Walker knocked on the front door. Lyra beckoned him in, and Kaden got him coffee and placed a clean plate on the table beside it.

"Here, take my seat. I was just leaving, and there's plenty of food left if you haven't eaten."

Lyra waved her hand across the table. "Help yourself."

Walker blinked and sat, shooting a wary glance at Kaden. "I hope I didn't interrupt something?"

"No, we'd finished eating," Kaden assured him as he tucked his jacket into a bag.

Walker frowned, clearly at a loss, but the smell of crisp bacon must have gotten to him because he loaded his plate and tucked in.

Lyra poured him coffee and topped up her own cup. "You're up early."

"I wanted to have a look around the park before too many people are out and about."

"Did you find anything?"

He took a large gulp of coffee, studying her over the rim.

"You did!"

"There were some boot marks in the bank by the stream in line with where we stood under the lamp."

"That's great."

He snorted. "Not so fast, Sherlock. It could be a clue but could also be from someone who was walking by the stream at an earlier time."

"Oh. I guess unlike dried blood or the temperature of a body, there's no timeline for footprints."

He smiled. "Depending on the weather, footprints can disappear slower than you'd think if they've been protected."

"So, the time frame looks good that this person was watching Raylene?"

"It's a long shot, but I took an impression of them."

"At least it's something. Well done."

An eyebrow disappeared under his hair. "Ah, it is my job."

"And I was just saying to Kaden that you're good at it."

"That's kind of you to say, and since I'm not used to the praise, I have to ask, what's got into you this morning?"

She sniffed. "What? A person can't be pleasant and encouraging?"

"A person can, but you aren't usually so encouraging, and not always pleasant if I'm honest."

"Well, I'm off." Kaden looked like he was fighting a grin as he kissed her cheek and shook hands with Walker. "Thanks for the hospitality and the tour of Fairview last night. I'll be in touch to find out if the two of you have solved the case." He left with a chuckle and a jaunty step.

"Funny guy," Walker said stiffly.

"Oh, he is that," she agreed. Something was different about Kaden, and it bugged her that she couldn't put a finger on it. "By the way, since I assume it wasn't on the off chance of a breakfast invite, what did you stop by for?"

"Just a courtesy call to make sure you and the others are all okay."

"I haven't seen Maggie, who is likely still in bed, or Mom, who's at the diner, but I'm fine."

"You look good." His checks flushed again. "I mean that there seems to be no ill effects from last night."

She had slept surprisingly well, putting it down to a couple of wines and sheer exhaustion, but he looked tired. "I'm fine. How about you? Do you think the murderer is hanging around?"

He wiped his mouth on a napkin and carried his dishes to the sink. "There's no way of knowing."

"If you're checking up on me, I think you have a good idea."

"I'm checking on everyone. In fact, I stopped by Raylene's and walked her to the diner. She seems okay, and now I'm off to check on Vanessa."

It sounded as if he were covering his tracks, but Lyra refused to read more into what he was saying. It was what he omitted that niggled at her. What had he found out about Ardie Loxhay? The department had ways of getting information, and it had been a couple of days already.

Maggie came out of her room, tying a dressing gown at her waist. "Did I miss another party?"

"Sorry, it was just Kaden leaving and the sheriff stopped by to check on us. Did we wake you?"

"Yeah, but for some reason, I'm starving, and that bacon has my name on it, so I forgive you all."

She reached across the table and, using her fingers, plucked a strip of bacon from the plate and munched on it with her eyes closed. When she was done, she opened them and stared at Walker.

"I've interrupted something, haven't I?"

"Not at all; I was just leaving. Thanks for breakfast." Walker put on his hat and touched the brim before strolling out the front door.

Maggie's jaw dropped. "You cooked him breakfast?"

"Actually, Kaden did."

"How civilized. Fancy all that testosterone in one room and no one got hurt."

Lyra moved the bacon from her reach. "Don't talk crazy. Tell me the truth. Have you and Mom been talking to Kaden about Sheriff Walker?"

Maggie frowned. "In what way?"

"In a romance kind of way."

"Not me." Maggie held out her hand. "Pinky swear."

"What about Mom?" Prepared to believe her, Lyra was about to link their little fingers.

Instead, Maggie snatched back the plate. "Patricia has her own code of ethics, and I'm not getting in the middle of a mother-daughter thing."

"I knew it," Lyra groaned. "Kaden was all weird this morning, and then he bounced out of here like he was off to a ball game."

"I don't get it."

"That's okay because I think I do." She sat back a little smugly. "Kaden has the idea that I like the sheriff, but the truth is, he likes someone, and he's trying to keep me and Mom off track so he doesn't have to tell us anything."

Maggie crunched thoughtfully on her bacon. "How the heck did you reach that conclusion?"

"I know that man like I know myself," Lyra explained. "He hasn't had a girlfriend in forever, and he wants to keep it to himself in case we disapprove. I can't think why, unless she's not good enough for him, in which case, why would he be thinking about dating someone like that?"

Maggie crammed in another piece of bacon before she answered. "Let me get this straight. Judgment aside on a woman we don't know, you're saying he thinks that if you have a shot with the sheriff, which by the way, sounds like a song, then he can be with whoever he's seeing in Portland because you won't nag him for details if you're all loved up?"

"Precisely—I think." Being loved up wasn't something she thought about. Well, not very often. Although, seeing Maggie and Dan together was triggering a little envy. A fact she wasn't about to admit to anyone.

"Well, well, well. I guess Kaden's smarter than I thought."

"I could think of another name for a friend who keeps secrets and knows darn well that Walker and I are not an item but is muddying the waters with it anyway. Anyway, how are we going to find out who this secret woman is?"

Maggie groaned. "Isn't one mystery enough for you?"

"It should be, but I don't make this stuff up." Lyra cleared the table, ignoring her friend's laughter. None of it was funny, and now she really needed to bake.

17

Once the kitchen was clean, Lyra and Maggie crossed the front lawn to the diner. She said good morning, made sure everyone was on track, and dodged questions that she couldn't answer. Patricia, as anticipated, had everything under control, freeing Lyra up to do other things.

"I'll be in the office if anyone needs me."

Maggie followed her. "If you're doing accounts this morning, I can help."

"Not right now, but I could use your help with something else. I need to get some hearing aids for Raylene ASAP. I saw the broken one in her bag last night, and it looked really old. Technology gets better every year, which makes me think that she needs testing to get a newer model, rather than getting them remade like they were."

Maggie's face lit. "There's a doctor in town that everyone says is wonderful. Most doctors have a list of good specialists close by they might recommend."

"That's a great idea and better than choosing randomly out of the phone book or traveling back to LA for replacements. It would be good if they were unobtrusive and easy to wear, as well as functional. In fact, anything that enables Raylene to adapt easily to them."

"I can see you've given this a lot of thought. I assume it's urgent."

Lyra nodded. "I see no reason to wait when it could be a hazard in the kitchen. Everyone should be able to hear if possible."

"I can't imagine not being able to." Maggie tilted her head. "She must read lips exceptionally well to deal with the noise in the diner as well as at the dinner last night."

Lyra was impressed by that as well. "The more I think about it, the more I feel sad that Raylene's had to pretend she could hear just to get a job. She would have been on the edge of a knife this whole time."

Her friend chewed her bottom lip for a moment. "It does suck. Leave it with me."

The wheels were in motion, and now Lyra's mind was free to work on necessary chores at the diner. Running through the inventory Leroy did regularly to make sure they had enough stock, the list of ingredients, as usual, refueled the urge to bake. It didn't matter so much what it was, but banana muffins sprang to mind. Cinnamon loved them, and they were a favorite with the knitting club.

Out in the kitchen she donned her apron and moved to the counter space reserved for her personal use and wiped it down. Collecting a large steel mixing bowl, she selected her ingredients. The recipe was entrenched in her mind, so there was no need for a paper copy.

Starting with sifting the flour, she added sugar and cinnamon. Naturally this was her favorite spice. In a separate bowl, she whisked eggs, buttermilk, and vanilla together, then stirred in the mashed bananas.

Making a well in the center of the dry ingredients, she poured in the banana mixture and melted butter, then gently folded them together until just combined.

Next she spooned the mixture into prepared muffin pans and placed a banana chip on the top of each one and placed them in the middle of the oven, setting the timer for ten to twelve minutes.

After cleaning down her space, Lyra handed Earl the dishes. This had to be the best perk of any chef's life when you owned a business and employed staff—no washing up!

When they were done and cooled, she sprinkled a little powdered sugar on them before placing the golden muffins on a tray which she carried out to the diner.

Raylene was behind the counter rearranging the display case, while Vanessa took orders from the knitting group.

"Hey, Lyra," Carrie-Ann called across the room. "Vanessa was telling us about last night."

Lyra frowned. Why would Vanessa embarrass Raylene by discussing the scene in the park?

Vanessa's mouth pinched as if she'd read Lyra's mind. "I hope you don't mind, but they were all interested in the food you served, and I couldn't help saying how amazing the dinner was."

Lyra had once again misjudged Vanessa. That had to stop. She was not her daughter or guilty by association. In fact, she worked hard, and had recently shown how kind she was. Placing her hand on the woman's shoulder, she smiled at the group. "Not at all. My staff deserved a treat, and it was a lovely evening. I'm just glad they enjoyed it."

"A fancy meal by a celebrity chef—you could charge a whole lot of money for that."

Lyra smiled. "That's not why I live in Fairview, Carrie-Ann."

"I suppose not, but if you ever want to give others that experience, and your prices aren't crazy, put my name down for it."

Finally finding a reasonable work-life balance, nothing could induce Lyra to have dinner parties for other than her friends and family, plus the odd one for staff. However, it was easier to jolly these ladies along rather than argue with them. "I'll bear it in mind."

"And me," June Edmondson chimed in. "My daughter in Portland says your boyfriend's restaurant is to die for. I'd love to try food like that."

Before she could say that Kaden was just a friend, Dot Stratten interrupted.

"Did you have fancy cutlery and get all gussied up last night?"

"It was in Lyra's home, which is lovely, and the table looked beautiful," Vanessa admitted. "I guess you could say we all dressed smartly, but not fancy. And she waited on us."

"Like a waitress? Can you imagine?" Dot said with awe.

"You don't have to imagine." Lyra laughed. "I've waited on you all at some stage."

"Pshh! In here is different. You're just doing a job."

Lyra shook her head at the strange logic. "I am lucky that I love my cooking and baking, but it still is a job, Mrs. Stratten."

"If you say so, dear."

There was no getting through to this lot, so Lyra left them to their discussion.

Maggie handed her a note as she came by the counter. "It's all sorted."

Lyra angled it away from Raylene and unfolded the paper.

Dr. Jenny Russo.
15 Main Street, Destiny.
Monday 10:00 a.m.

"Thanks, Mags. I'll tell her now. I hope she won't be offended."

"No way. This is an awesome thing, and I'm sure she'll be delighted to be able to hear properly."

Lyra hoped so. In her experience, people with little money could be so embarrassed when it came to help of any kind that they sometimes got angry.

"Raylene, could you come to my office for a minute?" Lyra saw the fear and smiled encouragingly. "You're not in trouble."

Relief flooded the server's face, and she nodded.

Lyra shut the door as soon as they were inside and motioned to a chair. "I have a gift for you with no strings attached, and I'd be obliged if you would accept it."

"A gift? Whatever for?"

"I can't fault your work, but you should be able to hear people the first time, so I'm getting you new hearing aids."

Raylene gasped. "But you can't. They're expensive, and I haven't worked here very long."

"Call it a loan if it makes you feel better." Lyra handed her the paper with the details. "There are no hearing specialists closer than Destiny, and this one was recommended by a local doctor. The appointment's been made, and I intend to drive you there on Monday. You will also be paid for the time off. I know this sounds bossy, but from a safety perspective, I need you to do this."

Raylene clutched her throat. "Gosh, I never considered that. I guess there is no choice then. Thank you so much, and I insist on at least doing extra hours to pay for them and will catch up the time off."

Lyra wanted to argue; however, she saw the pride in the woman's face and understood that this would seem like charity. "It's not necessary, but if you want to, then that's fine with me."

"Thank you. You don't know how much this means." Raylene swiped at her eyes and bustled out of the room.

Lyra sat back, satisfied with the outcome and appreciating that Raylene wasn't happy about being in her debt. This was understandable, yet necessary for all their sakes.

Raylene needed to be able to hear to prevent accidents in the kitchen, and it was even more important if there was someone in town who wanted to   hurt   her.

18

On the drive to Destiny, Raylene acted a little jittery, in that she fidgeted and kept looking behind them.

Lyra glanced in her rear mirror and with a jolt realized that the black van behind them had been there since the outskirts of Fairview. It didn't attempt to pass, and it wasn't tailgating. She picked up speed, and it fell back a little. That was good, except she didn't want to get a ticket and it wasn't as if they were on a secret mission, so there was no reason to assume they were being followed. Only, Raylene continued to fidget and glance in the wing mirror. "Is something wrong?"

"Pardon?"

"I asked if something's wrong?"

Raylene shook her head. "No. I'm just nervous about this new doctor and what she'll say about my hearing—and how much it will all cost. I remember how expensive my old ones were. They certainly won't be any cheaper after all this time."

"I told you not to worry about that for now."

"It's not easy to take help from people when you're used to going it alone."

There was something in the way she said this that made Lyra think she had reason to be suspicious, and a part of her understood that if something seemed too good to be true, it often was. Anything she said could be interpreted in that vein, but she gave it another try.

"Like I said, this is for safety purposes more than helping you out."

The raised eyebrow showed she didn't buy Lyra's motive.

"Okay, so it's for both reasons."

Raylene gave a short laugh. "I really am grateful, but you can't disguise that you're a good person or pretend that this isn't a big deal."

Embarrassed by the praise, when all she wanted was to do the right thing, Lyra couldn't shake the feeling that Raylene wasn't being totally honest about her problems. Problems that weren't all to do with being deaf. She decided that today they would deal with the hearing aids and tomorrow she would find out more about her server.

When they got to the doctor's, Raylene was immediately taken to an inner office. Lyra took a seat in the comfortable waiting room and pulled out her phone. Going straight to the notes, she found the latest recipes she was concocting. This meant that they hadn't reached a testing stage yet and were more a brain dump of which ingredients she thought would complement each other and ideas of how that might look.

Once she had a visual idea, she would try it out, then enlist Dan and Maggie to sample the dish—and now potentially Finn. (The name still sounded funny, even in her head.) After years spent together, she trusted the palates and opinions of Dan and Maggie. Many of the recipes they tried made it into her cookbooks, and it was time to start thinking about the next book. With the diner and a few other things she was considering, it would take many months to put it together.

The truth was she was always thinking of new recipes, but she'd been so busy lately that there had been little time to get anything on paper. A change of scenery and nothing pressing to take care of made this the perfect opportunity to do just that. The flowers on the reception desk fanned out in colored rows and reminded Lyra of a vegetarian lasagna. She had a recipe for that, but what if she used different vegetables than the ones that went into her usual one?

A man opened the door and looked around the room for a few moments, glancing at Lyra, then the receptionist who was on a call, before taking a seat in the far corner without checking in. Keeping his head down, he picked up a magazine and flicked through it a couple of times. Lyra tried to zone him out, but he seemed to be staring at her. Twice she looked up and his gaze slid away. It reminded her of paparazzi following her, then sneaking in places to get the gossip, and already worried about being followed, she was on her guard now. Moving to a new page in her notes and using the stylus, she drew the man as best she could—never professing to be an artist. What she hoped to capture was some features, but he wouldn't look up. However, he was noticeably well built, taller than average, and his hair was dark.

A door opened down the short hall, and the man shot up from his chair and exited the waiting room.

The receptionist glanced up, having not noticed him earlier. "Was he with you?"

Lyra shook her head, wondering if this was the breakthrough they needed.

The woman shrugged. "I guess he just realized he had the wrong room."

"Looks that way," she answered dubiously.

When Raylene came out of the doctor's room sometime later, she was beaming. Lyra had already paid, and she ushered her out to the car. "How did it go?"

Raylene put on her seat belt and turned in her seat. "The doctor was so lovely," she gushed.

"I'm so glad. Do you want to tell me what she said?"

"It was all good news." Raylene grinned and handed Lyra several sheets of paper. "These are today's tests and my last ones, which are on the database. My hearing hasn't gotten worse, and the new aids will be much smaller and more effective in distilling noises. Apparently, that will make it easier when I'm working or around a lot of different sounds. I tried a pair on, and although mine will be made for me, they were so small and comfortable, I already know they'll be a hundred times better than my old one. Plus, she's giving me exercises for tinnitus and some drops."

Lyra was trying to make sense of the lines and squiggles when her words sunk in. "Wait a minute. You only had one aid and now you'll have two? I thought your hearing wasn't any worse."

"It's not. In the bad ear, I'll have a transmitter, which will send sounds from that side of my head to my good ear. That way both ears kind of hear, and that will also help the tinnitus."

"Wow, that's clever."

Raylene nodded. "Technology is always moving, and before today, I thought that wasn't such a good thing."

Lyra laughed. "I know exactly what you mean. How long before you get the new ones?"

"They take about one to two weeks, and they'll ring to say they're ready."

"That's not a bad wait." Lyra nodded, but her mind was focused on the black van behind them once more. "I'm gasping for a drink. Let's stop off at a cafe I know and get takeout coffee."

"Only if I can buy," Raylene said firmly. "If you don't mind," she added.

"I don't mind at all." Stopping at the cafe could prove that they were being followed if the van also stopped. Hopefully if that happened, the driver might reveal himself to be the man in the waiting room, a.k.a. park man, because that couldn't be a coincidence.

Luckily there was a space right out front of the café, and when Raylene went to the counter, Lyra chose a table close to the door, burying most of her face behind the menu.

"Sorry, did you want food as well as coffee? I got takeout like you said."

Lyra peered over the top, where a confused Raylene obstructed her view of outside. "No, I'm good, thanks. Take a seat for a minute, would you?"

Raylene slipped onto the seat beside her and placed the coffees on the table. "Is something wrong?"

"To be honest, I think there is. Give it a minute, then I'll explain on the way home."

Picking at the plastic lid, Raylene glanced around the cafe nervously, while Lyra eyed the door. It remained closed.

After a couple of minutes, Lyra stood. "Come on, let's go." On her way to the car, Lyra looked up and down the street. The black van was nowhere in sight, which did nothing to ease her mind. Back on the road, Lyra watched behind them. Still nothing. After her effusiveness, Raylene was tellingly quiet, and Lyra decided this was as good a time as any to get to the truth. "Do you know who's following us?"

Raylene gulped. "Not really."

"I'm afraid that's not a good enough answer. You knew the man in the park was working for Ardie, didn't you?"

The gasp was loud. "How did you find out?"

"You just confirmed it."

Following a long silence, Raylene sniffed. "I'll pack up and leave Fairview as soon as we get back."

Lyra's eyes narrowed. "You know the sheriff won't allow it, and to what purpose?"

"You'll be safer."

"Is that so?" Lyra said stiffly. No matter how much she wanted that for everyone, including the rest of her staff and family, she couldn't believe that Raylene leaving would achieve it—not after everything that had happened. "You have to know that none of us will be safe until the killer is caught?"

After some hesitation, Raylene nodded. "There was a moment after you found Ardie's body when I thought it was over, but you're right. Until he's stopped, this isn't going to end."

"Because whoever he was working for is using you to get to me?"

Raylene nodded again and sighed. "I'm not who you think."

"I think you'd be surprised, but what I think doesn't matter. You need to tell me the truth—all of it."

"You deserve that, but if I tell you, I'm afraid something bad will happen."

"Something bad already did." Lyra's voice grew harsh. "A man died."

A sob ripped from Raylene's throat. "I tried to tell myself that Ardie isn't worth my pity, but it makes me sick to my stomach every time I think of it and see his angry face and the blood."

Lyra slammed on the brakes, and they slid to the side of the road, lucky that no other cars were around. Dust settled on the windscreen, and Lyra white-knuckled the steering wheel with both hands. "We are not moving an inch until you start from the beginning. You promised to be truthful, remember?"

White-faced and shaking, Raylene took several deep breaths. "I was a reporter for a small paper and tired of getting overlooked for promotion because I'm a woman. A year ago, I wrote a story that I didn't do enough research on because I knew what I had written would sell papers. When the truth came out, it blew up in my face. The paper I worked for fired me, and the person the article was about threatened me with jail. The court case was taking ages to come to trial, and I was broke because no one would hire me. Word gets around. Then Ardie came to me and said he could make it all go away."

"If you gave him a scoop about me? Something controversial and salable," Lyra prompted sharply.

Tears coursed down Raylene's cheeks as she nodded. "Ardie gave me a thick file on you which wasn't flattering. I didn't want to do it, but I was scared and said yes. When I was free to leave, I packed up and ran away. That's when I got the job in a diner on minimum wage because I had no experience. I could have made it work, but Ardie found me."

Her voice shook with fear, and Lyra waited while she composed herself.

"I had cheap accommodation a couple of miles from town and walked home at night. I'd begun to feel safe. I turned a tree-lined corner, and he was there waiting for me. I yelled and struggled, but there was nobody to hear me, and he was so strong. That's when my hearing aid got broken. He bundled me into a black van where the man from the park was. I don't know his name, but with both bullying me, I knew it was a case of doing the job, or as Ardie put it, jail would be something I wished for."

Lyra handed her a packet of tissues, remaining silent while Raylene calmed down. Meanwhile, it occurred to Lyra that they were sitting there like potential roadkill, and she slammed the car into gear. "I think we need to get out of here, but you keep talking."

They both kept an eye out for the van while Raylene continued.

"As scared as I was, believing some of what they said made it easier to apply for the job at the diner, but once I'd done my own research and after only a day hearing Maggie and Patricia talking about how the diner came about, I knew for sure it was all lies. When I overheard the knitting ladies talking about how you tried to help Poppy, I knew I couldn't go through with the article. Every person I spoke to at the diner and the few reporter contacts that still talk to me only had good things to say. Plus, I've never seen you do anything remotely underhand or mean, and you're not focused on money. You treat people the same, cook great food, and look after your staff." She grimaced. "Which meant I had nothing to give them."

"But they continued to put pressure on you to fabricate lies, and Ardie Loxhay hung around Fairview to get the evidence straight from you."

Raylene nodded. "Ardie said it was all about momentum and I had one more chance to get a real scoop. They wanted it bad. That's when I knew that whatever happened, I would be their patsy."

"So, you weren't responsible for the articles in the *Fairview Gazette*?"

"No!"

She was so adamant that Lyra begrudgingly believed her. Not for the first time since trouble began brewing, the wheels whirred in her mind, and suddenly a gear dropped into place. Raylene had seen blood, and she could only have done that if she was there. "You met with Ardie by the stream the day he died, didn't you?"

The woman gulped. "How did you know?"

"I saw you that day, remember? You were arguing with the man from the van. Raylene, I must know—did you kill Ardie Loxhay?"

"No!" she sobbed. "I swear it was an accident. We argued and he fell and hit his head, but that's it."

Lyra almost swung the car into the ditch when her feet hit the brakes for the second time. The shock and horror appeared to be real on Raylene's face and must mirror her own. They both took several deep breaths.

"You have to come clean to the sheriff."

"What if he doesn't believe me?"

"He will. Granted it may take some time and deeper investigation, but the truth always comes out. If you continue to try to hide the evidence, which is what you're doing, it will end very badly."

"I'm so scared that it will end badly no matter what I do. Ardie was murdered, but no one knows why, and that's eating me up inside."

"That troubles me too," Lyra admitted. "What about the murderer? Has he been in contact?"

"I switched my phone off so neither of them could get in touch with me. I haven't spoken to anyone since before Ardie died."

"Oh, Raylene. All that's likely done was make him angry and more determined."

Instinctively they both checked behind them. With no vehicles in sight, Lyra pulled back on the road. "Let's get home and locate Sheriff Walker right away, and don't for a minute think we've seen the last of whoever is following us."

"I'm sure you're right. All I hope is that after what happened with Ardie, that I'm the only focus now."

Lyra had already gone down that track in her mind and was convinced that she was in as much danger, if not more, than Raylene. After all, she was the reason for a plant in her diner. Someone wanted to hurt her—and it seemed that they were growing more desperate to do so.

Raylene was simply a tool to get to her.

19

Lyra drove straight to the police station and parked around the back, so no one would know they were back in Fairview. Along with Raylene, she sidled to the front door and once inside moved as far back from the glass as possible.

Janie Moore, nose deep in another of her romance books, glanced up with a frown.

"Oh. Hi, Ms. St. Claire and Ms. Dwyer." Quickly she stuffed the book under a pile of papers and gave Raylene a curious once-over.

"Hello, Officer. Is the sheriff in?"

"Let me check."

Janie left the hall door open, and they heard his deep voice, then the scrape of a chair.

"I wasn't expecting you." His voice was relatively warm until he saw their faces. He swiped a card across a pad attached to the door to the waiting room and beckoned them inside. "You better come down to my office."

The door automatically closed and locked behind them. Janie followed, but Walker stopped her at his office door.

"You should watch the desk, officer. I'll handle this query."

"Yes, sir." Janie bit her lip but did as he asked.

Walker closed his door and indicated that they should sit in the two straight-backed chairs in front of his desk. "Neither of you look happy, and I'm guessing this isn't a courtesy call."

"We were followed to Destiny and back," Lyra told him in a surprisingly clear voice.

"By whom?"

"We have no idea."

"What about plate numbers?"

Lyra grimaced. "Sorry, by the time I thought of that they'd disappeared."

He leaned back and steepled his fingers. "I see. It's not much to go on."

"I did do a drawing of one of the occupants." Lyra handed over her phone after locating the picture. "At least I think it is. He followed us into the ear specialists but left quickly and without seeing anyone. As you can see, I'm no Rembrandt."

A twitch at the side of his mouth was the only indication he was in any way amused.

"I'm not sure what I can do with this. Is there anything else?"

Lyra nodded to the woman fidgeting beside her. "Go ahead."

"I knew the man in the park," Raylene blurted, appearing smaller than she was, as she all but cowered in the chair.

His eyes narrowed. "When I questioned you about him, you said you didn't."

"If you recall, I said I wasn't sure." The words belied the desperation in her voice.

"Still a lie, am I right?" he asked tightly.

"Yes. I'm very sorry. I was scared of him."

Walker leaned forward and studied Raylene until she squirmed. "How about you start at the beginning, and let's have the whole truth this time."

Hands wringing in her lap and head bent, Raylene managed to repeat the story without breaking down until she got to what happened to Ardie. She was almost hyperventilating, and tears ran down her cheeks.

It had been just as hard to listen to a second time, and Lyra was struck by how much trouble Raylene was in. "Before she goes any further, shouldn't she have a lawyer?"

Walker hesitated for a moment, then sighed. "Yes. Let's do this right." He pressed a button on his phone. "Janie, please see if Karl Lowe will stop by as soon as possible."

"Some water might be a good idea too," Lyra suggested, thinking it was a timely opportunity for Raylene to take a break and calm down a little.

Walker raised an eyebrow but did as she asked. She noticed that he left the door open, and that the lunchroom was opposite them and empty.

"Karl is a good man and a great lawyer. You could do a lot worse."

Raylene gulped. "How am I going to pay for a lawyer?"

"You need one, which I should have considered before now, and I'll take care of it."

"But that's not fair." Tears began again in earnest. "After all I've done, and you don't know everything yet, I don't deserve your help."

"I'm pretty sure I know what happened." Lyra sighed. "And that you need Karl, so let's not argue about it."

"Everything okay?" Walker returned with a jug of water and glasses. He even poured for them.

"I was telling Raylene that Karl will do a good job for her and that it's just a precaution."

He eyed Raylene, but she was once more fixated on her fingernails, and it wasn't long before there was a knock at the door and Officer Moore made room for the lawyer to enter.

Karl had settled the claim for Dan when he'd been gifted the garage and a family member wanted to challenge the will. Soft-spoken, he kept to himself, much to the annoyance of several woman who considered him one of the most eligible bachelors in town.

He gave her a friendly smile as the men shook hands. "Nice to see you, Lyra."

"And you, Karl. How have you been?"

"Enjoying this beautiful summer we're having. How about you?"

"Ahh, if you don't mind," Walker interrupted. "Thanks for coming so quickly, Karl, but it's not a social call. This is Raylene Dwyer, and if you both agree, it would save a heap of time if you could represent her."

Karl scratched his head. "Well, now. Before I consider that, I guess you should explain what's going on."

Lyra stood. "Shall I leave?"

"No! Please stay," Raylene begged.

Walker nodded at Lyra's questioning look and pulled another chair from the corner of the room up to his desk for Karl. With everyone seated, he addressed Raylene. "Could you please start at the beginning for Karl?"

At the gentler tone, she glanced up and nodded. "Of course."

Karl asked a couple of questions about how Raylene felt about divulging everything to the sheriff and what the ramifications were of not speaking to him privately.

For the first time, Raylene sat up straight and looked Karl in the eye. "I want it all out in the open so I can sleep at night. I swear, I did not kill Ardie."

"Very well, as long as you understand what I've said."

"I do, and thank you for being here."

Walker checked that they were done. "When you're ready, please continue."

Raylene wiped her hands down her skirt. "Ardie messaged me to say I had to meet him at the stream. He sent text messages every day—and each one was nastier than the one before. I should add that they're on my phone and I kept every one of them."

"Well done," Lyra exclaimed and received a frown from Walker. She would do well to keep quite if she wanted to remain in the room. Which she most certainly did.

"When I said I still had no dirt on Lyra, and that I thought he'd made a mistake about how bad she was, I made to leave. He grabbed me by the arm." Raylene lifted the sleeve of her blouse and showed them faint marks from a bruise. "I told him to let me go, but he

161

squeezed tighter and shook me like a rag doll. Thinking of how he was threatening everyone at the diner, I lost my mind and shoved him away with everything I had."

She fussed with her fingernails and smoothed the sleeves on her blouse. "By this stage we were near the bank. He slipped on the edge, then lost his footing altogether. As he fell, he hit the back of his head on a thick branch. I didn't actually see this as I was running away, but when he didn't follow, I looked back and all I could see was his shoes pointing to the sky. I crept back, not sure if it was a trick to lure me closer, but the sound as he fell was sickening and I had to check." She took a deep shaky breath, and Karl handed her the glass of water.

"That's when I saw the branch beside him, and I saw blood on it. He seemed to be unconscious, and there was blood behind his head, so I knew he was injured, but his chest rose and fell slowly. I went to help him, but the minute I got close enough he grabbed my wrist and started yelling that he'd make me pay for this. I yanked hard to get free, and the next minute he slumped back. This time I ran and didn't look back."

"Why didn't you call the paramedics?" Walker asked, his voice loaded with accusation.

Raylene gulped. "I thought he was pretending again. I was returning to work when I forced myself to go back to check on him, only he was gone and there was no blood anywhere. The ground had been churned up by our struggle, but when I got back it had an almost swept look about it, and even the branch had disappeared. I really did feel sick and couldn't contemplate work, so I ran home."

Lyra gasped as bits of the puzzle clicked into place. "That means someone else moved him. Although it shouldn't surprise me. After seeing the man in the park, who was definitely not Ardie, arguing with Raylene, and then those shadows in the van which indicates at least two people were inside., it makes sense. If the person who found him alive, but injured, didn't want paramedics and by default the police involved, maybe they thought killing Ardie was the best answer, and he didn't even have to move him far because the thicket was a perfect hiding place. I think it's feasible that the murder was supposed to be pinned on Raylene."

For a moment Walker watched her with narrowed eyes. "I need to check out that scene again." Then he turned back to Raylene. "And get your fingerprints. Was Ardie the one who devised the plan to ruin Lyra?"

She shook her head. "He approached me, but made it very clear that he was the heavy to get what his boss wanted. It was also clear that he was as frightened of his boss as I was of him."

Walker tapped his pen on a blotter that covered a third of his desk. "After he was murdered, what happened with regards to your job with Ardie and his 'boss'?"

Tears rolled down Raylene's cheeks unheeded. "I admit it was stupid to think I could go back to work and pretend nothing had happened, but I didn't know what to do. I haven't heard anything from them because my phone's been off since Ardie died."

Walker made a rude sound in his throat. "What about this second man?"

That addition of a whole new line of questioning from Walker made the interview go on for a long time until Karl interrupted.

"My client appears to be flagging, and I think there's only so many ways you can ask the same thing. Ms. Dwyer states that she wasn't aware that Mr. Loxhay was dead, and from what we've heard, she had nothing to do with the man's actual death. I suggest you let her get some rest, knowing you can call her in for further questioning."

Walker didn't look entirely convinced. "Bearing in mind everything you've told me, how do I know you won't leave town?"

Raylene rubbed a hand over her face. "You have my word. It used to mean a great deal, and I'd like it to do so again. Besides, where could I go that 'he' wouldn't find me?"

It took a moment or two for Walker to digest this. "Very well. You should stay close to work and your home and not wander anywhere on your own for the foreseeable future. I'll have a deputy keep an eye on both of you."

Paler than ever, Raylene nodded.

"Please leave me your phone, Ms. Dwyer, and we still need to talk about your part in all this, Ms. St. Claire."

"Of course. You know where I'll be, unless you want to speak to me now?"

He hesitated, then shook his head. "No, I'll stop by later once I get in touch with my deputies and do some checking on what I've just heard."

With that they were free to go, and even though Lyra assumed she wasn't a suspect, it was odd how good being outside felt. She took in a deep breath. "Would you like me to drive you home?"

Also experiencing the delight of being out in the fresh air and possibly relief at her freedom, Raylene breathed deeply as well. "Could I come to the diner? I'd rather work, unless you don't want me there."

Did she? Lyra wanted Raylene to be innocent of everything, but she wasn't. Should she trust that this was indeed a woman who was browbeaten and more, until she felt there was no choice? Her intuition told her she should, only that had also let her down a few times. "Have you told the truth—about everything?"

The woman lifted a hand. "I swear."

Lyra searched her face, then nodded. "Well, I've backed you this far. I don't intend to stop now unless something comes to light."

Raylene blushed. "I don't know how to thank you."

"All I ask is that you keep telling the truth. Especially if someone contacts you—I need to know, and so does the sheriff to keep us all safe."

"Right now, that's all I want, and I promise, you'll be the first I tell."

Not being guilty of killing Ardie had solidified enough in her mind that Lyra chose to take Raylene's word for the rest of it, if she was going to let the woman stay at the diner in an attempt to keep her safe. How she got into these predicaments, she didn't rightly know, but was darn sure that no one would mess with her staff or her business for a second time and get away with it.

20

There was no denying Lyra was scared. The more Raylene told them, and then putting some of the pieces together, it showed her that there was every reason to be frightened. It was a small reassurance that a deputy would watch over them, but he couldn't be in all places. Unless Raylene slept at the farmhouse and they closed the diner, there was ample opportunity for this madman, whoever he was, to get to them. He'd threatened, blackmailed, and murdered to get to Lyra, proving that he wouldn't stop at any barrier.

After coming back to the diner and throwing herself into cooking to give herself a little time to mull things over, Lyra wanted—no, she needed to talk to someone impartial. As impartial as a person could be once they heard the whole story thus far.

By an unspoken agreement, neither she nor Raylene told the team about today's happenings other than the good news over the hearing aid. Lyra would have to come clean with Patricia, Maggie, and the others about being followed, but first she had to think of a way to tell them. Some would want Raylene gone from the diner, but surely others would sympathize with the woman. To keep the peace, she might need to go along with the majority, and she wasn't prepared for that yet.

Informing Maggie that she was going to the farmhouse for a short break, Lyra nodded at the deputy standing in the walkway, and with Cinnamon trotting beside her, rang Kaden as soon as she was out of earshot.

He answered the video call, a silly grin plastered on his face, just as someone moved out of view from beside him. "How are you, Chef? Still hunting down a murderer?"

Lyra glanced around the veranda of the farmhouse and hurried inside with Cinnamon, closing and locking the door behind them. "You could say that."

"I don't like the way you say that. What's wrong?"

She shrugged and propped her phone up against Maggie's latest floral center piece on the table so she could rub Cinnamon's head. "I'm just frustrated and confused. It turns out that Raylene did know the dead man after all. She's been threatened by him and blackmailed into writing some sort of exposé on me."

"The paparazzi strike again, just as you suspected," he growled.

"You have no idea how I wish I was wrong. I'd been doing some research, but I kept hitting blank walls with Ardie. Maybe Walker will find out more with the detailed description Raylene gave of the other guy in the park."

He leaned closer to the screen. "Do you still trust her?"

"If I'm honest, a good deal less than I did a day ago, but I've allowed her to keep working for now because I think she'll be safer around people. I also think she's innocent of the murder."

"Do you? Handling the truth so loosely won't have endeared her to anyone there, but until you know if she's innocent of anything more serious, it's a good way of keeping your enemies close."

"That's kind of what I had in mind, but I haven't yet told my team what happened today, and it's hanging over me."

Kaden frowned. "You know they won't be impressed by her or you for not telling them already, and they'll want more answers."

"That's my problem. I simply don't have enough answers, and I'm already exhausted by the thought of trying to explain what I do know. You know what Mom's like."

He nodded. "Like a terrier, which is only because she loves you."

Her lip trembled. "I know."

"What about Walker? He must have completed his research on the dead guy by now and found out who he works for."

"I would have thought so, but if he has, he's not telling me."

"He's the law, and from what we've both witnessed, they have to be cagey about this information."

"Selective is a better word. Sometimes I think he's telling me everything, and at others I know darn well he's not."

"I guess he could be trying to spare you a little worry."

She raised an eyebrow. "It surprises me that you'd stick up for him this way."

"He might be an officer of the law, but he also seems to be an upright guy. For the most part."

"Do I detect a little bromance seeping in?"

His nose wrinkled. "Funny lady. Although, we did chat a bit the other night, and I've changed some, not all, mind you, of my thoughts on him. He seems to care about Fairview and its residents a great deal. Including you."

It was a little weird for Kaden to be so generous about the sheriff. However, she'd been just as wary about Walker when they first met. Now that he'd grown on her, it was almost natural that Kaden would also adjust his opinion. "Like you said, it's his job. I just wish I knew why someone is out to get me and, going forward, what doing so might entail. Strangers come into the diner all the time. If Ardie's boss hired someone else to finish the job, I'd have no idea if it was a customer, would I?"

"If you're being followed, that indicates that he already has someone else in town."

She nodded. "Or more than one. I couldn't see clearly into the car, but there were two shadows in the front, and then there's the guy from the park and the specialist. We're pretty sure that he at least is one and the same, but who really knows?"

"Let Walker deal with this," he pleaded. "It's too dangerous for you to be poking around like a bear with a stick in a beehive."

She sighed heavily. "I hear you."

"Then why do I get the impression it won't make a blind bit of difference what I say if you get it into your head to do some poking?"

She smiled. "If anyone can talk me out of something, it is definitely you, my friend."

"Hmm. We'll see. I won't hold my breath. Look, I'm sorry, but I must go. I'm a chef down tonight."

"Do you need me?"

He smiled gently. "Thanks for the offer; even if I don't believe you'd be silly enough to leave town with the investigation hanging over you, but we're well staffed at present. And midweek is slower, which makes it the perfect time to give Angie more training in the kitchen."

The young waitress Lyra met a few months ago had shown so much passion for cooking that Lyra let her work in her restaurant while Kaden's was being rebuilt after a fire. Now Kaden was giving her another chance to prove herself, which was wonderful. "How is she doing?"

"Really well. Of course, I can't tell her that in case she gets a fat head." He laughed and ducked as something landed on his desk.

She was pleased to see he was happy and having fun with his staff. Somebody should be. "I better get back to the diner and explain what's going on. Thanks for listening to me and my troubles again."

"A trouble shared is a trouble halved," he reminded her. "Please be careful." He blew a kiss before shutting off the call.

"We are so lucky to have such good friends," she told Cinnamon, already feeling a little lighter. Of course, everything was better after talking to Kaden, and with her team to face, she'd needed that boost. She'd also been reminded that some of them followed her through so much already.

After the dinner rush and before Vanessa was due to leave, she called them together. Patricia was supposed to go home as usual and then come back for the meeting, but with her worry radar switched to high alert, she'd hung around, and for safety reasons Lyra was glad. Maybe it was in her tone, because Dan had taken her call to come to the meeting seriously and was on time.

They stood around the kitchen table, and though it wasn't easy to begin, once Lyra did the story came rushing out. The result went just as Kaden predicted. There were a ton of questions and everyone eyed Raylene warily. To be fair the woman didn't hide from the accusatory looks and in a quivering voice answered as best she could.

Eventually Lyra put up a palm. "Okay, I know what a shock this is, but Raylene has had a rough time of things to get her to this point. We don't know how any of us would react in the same situation, so it would not only be kind to give her the benefit of the doubt but would also help us get through this."

No one spoke for a couple of minutes, which is a very long time when you're waiting to see which way the wind will blow.

Finally, Vanessa broke the silence. "If this is the sum of everything that's happened until now, then we must look out for each other, including Raylene. However, I shall be furious if I see anything more about me or Poppy in any paper."

"I wouldn't do that," Raylene said through trembling lips. "It honestly wasn't me who gave those articles to the *Gazette*."

"Are we all okay with Raylene continuing to work here?" Lyra pressed, wanting to nip things in the bud. She wasn't shocked by the lackluster nods and couldn't blame them for being wary. As far as she was concerned, it was a good enough place to leave

171

things for today, and Raylene could hardly expect a better response.

"Thank you, everyone. Dan, would you mind driving Raylene home please and make sure she's locked in?"

His face said he'd rather not, but Dan was a gentleman. "Will I take you too, Vanessa?"

She nodded and walked out with them a little stiffly. It was going to be awkward around here until this was resolved, but Lyra watched her team leave and was pleased that she hadn't misjudged them.

21

Lyra was at the kitchen table working at her laptop when Walker arrived at the farmhouse a couple hours later. Cinnamon growled until she saw who was at the door, then shook her butt until he bent to scratch her back.

He gave a slight groan as he stood and stretched his back. "I hope you don't mind me coming by, and sorry it's so late."

"I'm glad of the company. Maggie's with Dan, and Mom's gone to bed. You must be exhausted too." No must about it when the lines around his eyes were etched into his skin.

"Probably no more than you." He rubbed a hand through his hair. "This was some day."

"It was, and yet I can't settle. Come sit at the table, and I'll make us fresh coffee."

"Coffee would be wonderful." He followed her across the room, and his stomach growled loudly.

She turned to see him blush a little. "Would you like a muffin? It's banana."

"What, no savory ones?" he teased.

"You never said if you liked them, so I figured you didn't."

He grinned ruefully. "I didn't want to admit how delicious they were. It seems truth has been hiding in all kinds of places."

"I couldn't agree more." Placing a plate with the muffin, a knifc, plus a small pat of butter in front of

173

him, she sighed. "Just when you think you can trust people again, lies bite you in the ankle."

At her frustrated tone, Cinnamon peered out from under Walker's seat.

"She knows when things aren't right with you," he said as he cut the muffin in half and slathered it with butter.

Lyra smiled. "It's hard on her when there's so much going on, but she understands more than people think."

"I agree."

"You do?" Walker had been skeptical when she first moved to town and had told him of the beagle's ability to read people.

"Don't look so surprised," he protested. "Not every dog is as intuitive as your beagle, and Cinnamon's shown how clever she is more than once."

Cinnamon banged her head on the chair and shot out between his legs, tail thumping.

"She never gets tired of hearing how clever she is." Lyra laughed, then stopped just as suddenly. The sheriff wasn't exactly visiting after all. She brought their coffees to the table and sat opposite him.

They both took a few sober sips, then he pulled out a pad and pen and nodded at her.

"You get started when you're ready. It might seem tedious, but memory can become clearer as you talk, and you may remember more now that you've had time to contemplate the series of events that led to today."

"A series of events," she mused, a little disappointed that he didn't find her revelation more interesting. "That's exactly what it's been like. From hiring Raylene, to finding the body, then the articles in the paper, which the new owner won't say where they came from."

"Yes, he did say you'd been to visit him."

She shrugged. "He clearly printed them on the say-so of his boss against his better judgment. I found out that Ardie worked for a number of papers, but he hasn't appeared for a while anywhere, and there's been nothing with his name attached in the *Fairview Gazette* ever."

Walker didn't comment on the new owner. "Ardie was obviously busy doing things other than reporting. What else are you working on?"

She wouldn't deny it, even to remove his long-suffering look. "I've asked Dan to look for vans in the area, to find out if anyone's seen the black one that's' been following us. We thought that with him working at the garage, he might hear something."

"You better leave that to my department. Those guys are not people you want Dan to have to deal with. Anything else?"

She didn't go into how Dan was in the army, and adept at hand-to-hand stuff, because Walker was right in that her friend shouldn't have to deal with henchmen. Only, Dan had offered, and at the time she wanted to clutch at any straw. She would speak to him tomorrow about letting that go.

Aware he was studying her; she licked her lips, which were suddenly dry. "I'm still trying to find out who submitted those articles to the *Gazette*. You haven't said, but given where Ardie came from, I think it's someone from LA, who has a lot of pull and even more money. There's this paper, the *LA Enquirer*, which had a decent reputation until a few years back. The editor there has been under scrutiny for a while for printing sensational stories with little foundation." She grinned wryly. "I even featured in a few of them. Who better to know people willing to make fake news than someone doing it themselves? And he's on a sabbatical." She leaned back with a sense of satisfaction.

Walker clicked his pen nonchalantly. "Would that be Roman Harper?"

"Yes! Don't tell me you already knew?" She rolled her eyes. "Of course, you did. Did you drag it out of Mr. Eckhart?"

"I'm the sheriff. People have to tell me stuff, so dragging isn't necessary."

"Do you know how he's connected with me?" she grumbled, annoyed by the slight smirk.

"Only regarding those articles Eckhart printed. We're also running the description of the man in the park, but so far no luck. It's a shame Raylene didn't get a name. Now, let's get back to the case, starting from finding the body." He'd pulled out her statement and ran his pen along it as she spoke, making notes in the margins.

As tired as she was, he was right: talking about it put things into perspective, and knowing that he was digging even deeper than she could eased her worries, just a little. However, there was something in the back of her mind that she couldn't put a finger on, but it was to do with the articles—she just knew it—and why she couldn't let it go.

In bed sometime later, Lyra tossed and turned as another question presented itself. From the perspective of the killer, and with her cover effectively blown, why was Raylene still here? She shuddered at the way Ardie had died, anxious that her server wouldn't meet the same fate, and in that moment two possible scenarios sprang to mind: (a) Raylene could still be used as the fall person, or (b) the game wasn't up yet. Of course, that posed third question–whose game was it?

Lyra wanted to believe it was a good sign that Raylene stayed to see this through and stand up for herself and the team. But what if staying was still a ruse to get the scoop on Lyra as she stumbled around another murder, making mistakes, and trusting the wrong people?

And if this owner was involved in more than forcing Lester Eckhart to print ugly stories, what was his motivation? It must be something big to gamble with his paper.

It made her stomach churn to think of the people who had already tried to harm her, but they had also formed a perception that she was a bad person who brought their wrath down upon herself. Slowly she spoke the names as if she were in *Game of Thrones* and discarded them one by one.

Symon Reeves, her ex-agent who was in jail. Cameron Willetts, a contestant in Portland who thought he should win all the competitions he entered and secure a place in Lyra's restaurant. He'd killed another contestant before turning his hatred to Lyra when his plan failed, and was in jail for a very long time. Phillip McKenna, the late Rob McKenna's son, was initially jealous at Dan accepting the garage gifted to him by Rob but had come to see he'd misjudged his father's friends. Poppy Fife, who couldn't afford to take care of her mom, Vanessa, and had stolen from Rob, then accidently killed him, and was also in jail.

Why did disagreements have to result in so much misery? She pummeled the pillow, causing Cinnamon to scramble to the end of the bed and stare accusingly.

"Sorry, girl. I'm okay, and you did nothing wrong," she said soothingly.

The beagle belly-crawled up the blankets to nuzzle Lyra's cheek, and she cuddled her girl close. "I guess it's obvious that Raylene simply has no choice, financially or otherwise—she must stay. If she ran, she wouldn't stand a chance on her own, but here we can stick together."

The beagle made a sound that Lyra chose to accept as agreement, and they lay snuggled together until Cinnamon yawned, stood, and walked in a circle until she had the position just so, then dropped into a ball at the foot of the bed and closed her eyes.

"Some companion you are. I was hoping you'd help me solve this."

One lazy eye opened, followed by another yawn, then shut again.

"Maybe tomorrow," she muttered, wishing she could fall asleep as easily.

She felt so responsible for the whole mess. Not that she'd made it happen, but she was certainly the catalyst.

She was about to nod off when she had another epiphany. While Raylene's hearing wasn't good in many situations, she did have an uncanny ability to know when a person entered the diner or was waiting at the counter.

Dragging her laptop from the side table, she looked up "senses" and found the information incredibly interesting. It explained much about how a person's other senses might kick in when one was lost.

22

Lyra yawned and stretched. With little sleep last night, she was running on empty. So, when half an hour after her shift started, Raylene was AWOL, Lyra's stomach began a war dance. Vanessa moped around the diner as if she'd been stabbed in the heart, and Leroy wore an I-told-you-so look, while Earl had never been so fascinated by dirty pots and pans.

After all the words and promises, this was not happening! Lyra groaned inwardly. "Things come up. She could have slept in or be unwell." *Darn it, she'd spoken aloud.*

Vanessa shook her head. "After last time? Raylene would have rung me or anyone else here if that were the case."

"Not if she's still asleep," Lyra suggested with a sliver of hope. "Yesterday was huge, and she could be exhausted. Why don't you try phoning her?"

Vanessa brightened for as long as it took to make the call. "There's no answer on her cell, and she has no landline."

Her stomach clenched. This wasn't right, and Lyra had a strong urge to find out what the problem was. In fact, that urge couldn't be ignored. Walker didn't believe in coincidence, and in this instance she agreed. Sneaking away to her office, she tried to get hold of Walker with no luck. Janie picked up at the station but couldn't help except to say that the deputy watching Raylene's place had called in an hour ago to say that the house was still locked up.

Back in the kitchen, she untied her apron. "I think I'll go check what's wrong with Raylene," she said casually. "Cinnamon will be happy to have her walk early." Lyra would also feel safer with the beagle at her side.

Patricia wiped her hands on a towel, then clasped her hands in front of her. "You should ring the sheriff."

"I did. He's unavailable, and according to the report from the deputy watching her, Officer Moore says Raylene is still home. If she's sick, she might need a doctor."

A hum emanated from Patricia. "I'm against this, but I can see you've made up your mind. You should go around the road and stay out of the park."

"It's daylight, Mom."

"It was daylight when you found the body," Patricia reminded her. "Which means the time of day is irrelevant to the people who want to hurt Raylene—and you."

"We don't know that anything's happened to her, and there is a deputy on duty at her house to make sure she's safe," Lyra objected, despite the sinking feeling in the pit of her stomach. Like Vanessa had said, if Raylene was sick, she would have phoned by now.

As if reading her mind, Patricia stood hands on hips, in Lyra's way.

"Okay, I'll go around the street instead of the park, but it will take me longer."

"Better to be gone longer than not get there at all." Patricia sniffed. "And make sure you touch base with the deputy and make him call the sheriff if things don't look right."

Lyra hadn't seen her mom this agitated for a while, and it would be better not to try her patience. "You're right, and I will be extra careful."

Patricia raised an eyebrow. "Maybe Leroy should come with you."

"He's got too much to do here," Lyra protested.

"I'll come." Maggie grabbed her bag and stood by the back door, determination written in every line of her body.

This seemed to be reluctantly agreeable, so Lyra threw her apron on the table and ushered Maggie outside before there were any more objections. Outside, Cinnamon joined them, and the little group headed down the alleyway.

They hadn't got far when Maggie sighed. "You know I want to support you, but are you sure we should be doing this instead of waiting to hear back from the sheriff? I think he'd prefer it."

Lyra turned to face her. "To be honest, I don't think there's time to wait, Mags. I have a bad feeling, but you don't have to come."

"And let you go on your own when you have bad vibes? I don't think so. Besides, If I hadn't offered to come with you, there may have been a mutiny in that kitchen."

Lyra appreciated that Maggie was trying to lighten the mood. "So, accompanying me was all a ruse to get out of there and not for my protection after all."

"See it how you want. I prefer to think of this as a nice walk with my friend and boss who is cooking up something that I can't eat, and she probably shouldn't be mixing anything together in the first place." They continued to walk, and a heavy silence grew.

Maggie groaned. "There's more to this than just your fear for Raylene, right?"

Lyra decided it would be nice to get a few things off her chest, and Maggie often had good insight. "That's foremost on my mind, but I did happen to come across something last night that could make sense of what happened to Ardie."

"I'm listening." Maggie wrinkled her nose. "Although I'm not sure I want to."

"Raylene is deaf," Lyra continued. "At least partially, right?"

"Do you think she's lying?"

"No, that's not it. I paid for the tests and saw the results. She is deaf in one ear and struggles with the other. So, she can't hear that well, but she can feel."

Maggie frowned. "What do you mean?"

Lyra wasn't explaining this well, and she tried again. "It's not unusual for deaf people to have their other senses heighten. Sometime a great deal. I've been researching it, and apparently vibrations can help with things like traffic or people approaching. At the park, Raylene fought off Ardie and had her back to him when he fell. She didn't know or couldn't know how he hit his head or on what if she had to rely on hearing, right?"

She frowned, then grabbed Lyra's arm. "But she 'felt' him fall."

Lyra nodded, pleased that Maggie was on the same wavelength.

Suddenly, Maggie pointed ahead. "She's going the wrong way."

Cinnamon had run ahead, looking back to check they were following, and now had darted down the path through the park. Lyra called the beagle, but she didn't return.

"It might be a good idea if before we go to Raylene's we take a look at the spot again."

Maggie chewed her bottom lip for a moment. "Patricia will be furious, but I guess we'll be safe together."

They hurried down the path, Lyra aware she was breaking a promise. The tape was gone from the scene, but she still stepped carefully to the place Raylene had said Ardie fell, making sure Cinnamon stayed by her side. "There's no branch near here and nothing large enough to cause the knock to the head I saw. Let's assume for a moment that the murderer was there all the time, watching and waiting. He saw Raylene come back to check and then run off."

Maggie waited a few feet away, and now she gasped. "After she left the second time, he dragged Ardie off and killed him."

"It's one possibility." Lyra nodded. "The point is why kill Ardie at all if he was doing the job of his heavy? And where is the branch or rock Ardie hit his head on? It had to be big enough to make him go down, but light enough to get rid of the evidence. My guess is that he threw whatever it was in the stream. I remember that it rained heavily the night before and the stream was moving faster than usual. A rock would drop to the bottom, but a branch would likely float."

Maggie gasped and grabbed Lyra's arm for the second time. "A branch floats!"

Lyra unfurled her friend's fingers, wondering if Maggie had gone mad, because there would surely be a bruise. "A small one would. Isn't that what I just said?"

"No, you don't understand. I found a branch on the other side of the stream and took it to the farmhouse."

Lyra gasped. "Oh my gosh! You made a centerpiece for the table with it."

"Do you really think it could be the same one?" Maggie grimaced. "I didn't see any blood. Apart from a bit of weed from the stream, it was nice and clean and just needed drying out for a few more hours before I could dress it."

They were both horrified. They'd sat at a table eating and drinking possibly with the evidence in front of them all the time.

After a few minutes, Lyra took a deep breath. "Listen, we can't be certain about what happened. We'll go to Raylene's as planned and then see the sheriff after that and explain our hypothesis."

They trudged up the path and into the lane. There was no sign of a deputy, and at the small house, the curtains were closed.

Lyra knocked, increasingly louder to no avail. "I'm going around the back."

"Not without me."

Maggie kept close, and together they rounded the corners of the house until they were behind it. The tiny backyard needed mowing, but there was nowhere for a person to hide. With a small sigh of relief, Maddie led the way to the back door.

She reached out for the handle, and Cinnamon growled.

23

The hairs on the beagle's back stood upright, as did the ones along Lyra's arms.

The door stood ajar.

"Hello? Raylene," Lyra called from outside. Silence was the only answer, until Cinnamon whined and nudged Lyra's hand. "You'd better call the police." When she took a step over the threshold, Maggie grabbed her again and pulled Lyra back. This was getting to be a habit, but in all honesty, she did need a second to get her shaking under control.

Maggie had her phone ready but didn't let go of Lyra. "You can't go in there. This is just like those movies where the innocent bystander does a stupid thing like go inside a place that something bad happened in, and the audience is screaming for them not to."

"She may be injured and need our help," Lyra told her reasonably.

The call connected, and while Maggie spoke urgently to whoever answered, Lyra slipped from her grasp and went inside. With another soft whine, Cinnamon followed.

"Find Raylene," Lyra urged as she moved cautiously across the kitchen.

The beagle went around her and set to work. The place was small, and there weren't many opportunities for a person to hide. Still, Lyra kept her back to the wall and moved through the sitting room to the bathroom. Cinnamon whined louder, and Lyra had to steal herself to open the door. Raylene was there! In the bath—fully clothed. The water was up to her chest stained a deep red.

Lyra gulped several times, patting the whimpering beagle. "Good girl. Go find Maggie." For one of the few times, Cinnamon disobeyed. She barked loudly down the small hall, then went to sit by the far wall, watching her intently.

So be it. Lyra felt for a pulse, relieved when she found it, albeit a faint one. Grabbing towels, she wrapped them around Raylene's wrists, securing them tightly with the belt from a dressing gown hanging on a peg, which she managed to rip in half. The water was warm. She yanked the plug from the bath. Somewhere she'd read that warm water made the blood flow more freely, and she made sure to raise both Raylene's arms well out of the water, hoping the elevation would help as well. As an afterthought she imagined that the poor woman would get cold soon, and too scared to manhandle her out of the bath, draped the gown across her once the water was gone.

Footsteps hurried through the house, and Walker burst through the doorway. Crouched low, he pointed a gun at her. She raised an eyebrow. "We're the only ones in here. Call the paramedics. Raylene's slit her wrists but is alive."

Relief and anger rippled his features, but he holstered his weapon and gave instructions to a deputy to search the rest of the place before making the call. Lyra took one of Raylene's hands in hers and patted it gently. "It's okay, Raylene. We've got you."

A couple of fingers moved, and Lyra clasped them harder. Suddenly she felt something pressing into her hand. Gently, she turned Raylene's hand over and opened her own to reveal a piece of cloth.

"Walker! Look, she has something in her hand. It looks like material—from a shirt?"

He slid across the tiled floor. "Where did she get it?" As he asked the question, he removed a plastic bag from his pocket and, turning it inside out, placed it over the cloth, carefully tilting Raylene's hand so that it dropped inside.

Lyra glanced at the woman's face before focusing on Raylene's broken fingernails. "I would say the material came from the person who did this to her and left her for dead. She must have fought back. Look at the bruise on the side of her head."

He leaned in closer and made a whistling sound through his teeth. "Darned if you aren't right."

A siren wailed close by just as Raylene opened her eyes. "He won't stop," she rasped.

"Who won't stop?" Walker demanded.

She lifted her hand fractionally and then it slumped back, her eyes closing once more.

Lyra gulped. "She's lost a lot of blood. I hope she'll be okay."

"You've done as much as you can, and probably saved her life," Walker said softly, then pulled her away so the paramedics could get by.

It was such a small room that it proved necessary for them to wait outside, where Maggie hugged Cinnamon as if she would never let her go, especially after Lyra explained what had happened.

Walker finished on a call and came to speak to them. "I'd appreciate you keeping this to yourselves for now. Raylene's place is a crime scene, and for all we know there are other clues. We need to ascertain whether our suppositions are correct before we go any further down the road of murder."

"We won't say anything, but you heard it straight from Raylene. Someone did this, and they will want to finish the job they started."

"I was there too," he reminded her, "but she was barely conscious."

"And the material?"

"It could be from something of hers."

Lyra shook her head. "You don't believe that and neither do I."

"It doesn't matter what anyone believes. The process is to look at each situation from a variety of angles, and we must trust that process."

"I know. Only it's hard to contemplate suicide with that evidence. Speaking of which, did you ever get the threatening messages she received?"

"You never forget anything, do you?"

She shrugged. "Not if I can help it."

"I read them, and they were as she said. Unfortunately, the phone records pointed to the number of a burner phone."

"But they can be traced, right?"

"Only regarding where it was purchased, data usage, and the location that it was used. It's something, but not enough to say it wasn't purchased by anyone other than Ardie because it was paid for in cash and used only locally."

Disappointed, Lyra shivered in her damp clothes and then was horrified as she looked down at herself and saw the blood on them and her hands, which she wiped on her pants.

"Is it okay if we head back to the diner? When you need our statements, you could get it from us there, and I desperately need to change."

"As long as that's exactly where I'll find you. Don't go all CSI on me, you hear?"

"Yes, Sheriff."

Lyra strode back around the house with Maggie and Cinnamon running to keep up.

"Are you okay, Lyra?"

"No. I'm frustrated, and angry."

"With the sheriff? As far as I can tell, he's just doing his job."

Lyra stopped suddenly, causing Cinnamon to bump into her legs. "Not with him. With me. If only I'd made sure she wasn't alone, I might have stopped this from happening." She shook her head. "I guess I'm more shook up than I thought."

"No wonder you are. Finding her like that must have been awful, and yes, earlier would have been better, but Raylene would have been a goner if you hadn't decided to go to her house when you did. Focus on that."

Lyra's lips quivered. "I just hope we were in time. She was so pale, and there was so much blood."

Maggie threw an arm around her shoulder. "Give yourself a break. You saved her life, sure as I'm standing here. I'll ring the hospital as soon as we get back and keep ringing until we hear how she is."

"Thanks, Mags. I also feel guilty for doubting her, which I've done so many times."

"Me too. However, we had reason enough to do that, and thanks to you, we can tell her we're sorry because she's alive."

Cinnamon danced at their feet, trying to get in on another hug, and Lyra managed a weak half smile. Maggie had said the same thing three times, so she was going to listen and try to get some perspective on this.

"Come on; I need coffee and a place to sit down."

"Me too. I'd also like to understand why scaring the life out of me makes me hungry."

Lyra was surprised when her own stomach grumbled. Maybe that was a good sign, that all would be well.

Neither of them wanted the likely grilling they'd be subjected to from everyone at the diner, including the customers when word got out—if it hadn't already. So, Lyra took Maggie's next suggestion that they head to the farmhouse instead; she had a quick shower while Maggie made coffee and pulled out the container of cookies.

Sitting opposite each other at the large kitchen table, Lyra stared into her mug for several minutes, lost in the recollection of what they'd been through, the cookies disappearing as if by magic.

Maggie looked over her cup. "This is eating you up."

"That's an understatement." Lyra sighed. "Walker is undoubtedly looking into everyone connected with this case, but he isn't sharing all that information with me. I trust him, but if it was so easy to kill Ardie and then attempt to kill Raylene, it stands to reason I'm next on his list."

"Because he can't get what he really wants, which is to ruin you?"

"I think that might have been the starting point, but the endgame has changed, and I need to know why."

"Most people would wait to find out, rather than incite the person responsible." Maggie groaned a little. "But you certainly aren't most people."

"I'm not sure if that's a compliment or not." Lyra offered a wan smile.

"Me either, but you know I'll do anything to help."

No matter what mess Lyra found herself in, Maggie had never run away from the problem, and this was a doozie. "There is something. I found out that several months prior to his death, Ardie worked for a paper in LA. I did some research and found that he'd produced a couple of decent articles, but that was some time ago, and he isn't known for much else since then. Raylene also worked for a paper in LA, but a different one. Neither of them had particularly good-quality journalism."

"Did they know each other before this?"

"I think in that world they are all aware of each other, but not according to Raylene. Because she was targeted after falling on hard times and had a black mark against her name in the business, it makes sense to me that Ardie was in a similar situation until he fell off the radar. Although given his background of bullying, he potentially wouldn't require much persuasion. Anyway, that's my theory."

Maggie tilted her head. "The plot thickens."

"I know it's all suppositions, but it does make sense, right?"

"Absolutely."

"Good. That makes me feel less crazy." Lyra continued, "After being forced into the job through fear, according to Raylene, Ardie was instructed to pay her well for information that discredited me, but she wouldn't be responsible for writing the story on me and the diner. So, who would get that job?"

"Ardie?"

"While it may be egotistical to assume that this article would feature in a major paper and a renowned reporter would get the task, I just can't see how a top paper would use an unreputable source. Even a tabloid."

"Could they print it under a different name? Does that happen?"

"That's what I need you for. Do you still have any contacts in the journalism world?"

"I might. They'd all be friends of Symon's, your ex-manager, so they wouldn't be exactly top players. You can assume that they'll want something for the information if it's important enough."

"What could we offer? Money?"

"Seriously? If they were any good, they'd want an interview."

Lyra grimaced. "At this point, trading an interview for any leads would be worth it."

"Once you invite them back in…" Maggie shrugged.

"I know, it will be hard to back off again, but this isn't going away, is it?"

Maggie shook her head. "Not that I can see."

"Then there's no choice as far as I'm concerned. I'd ask Raylene about her contacts too, but she needs to get better first."

"Absolutely. I can't say I'm looking forward to talking with any of them."

"I know, and I hate to ask, Mags."

"It's fine. Thanks to Symon, I've had some experience with these kinds of people."

Lyra nodded. "Be careful. Take no unnecessary risks."

Maggie got straight on the phone.

24

While Lyra sat back and listened to her assistant's coercion, she thought of the poor woman who was by now in hospital. Raylene was stronger than she knew, but it was sickening to think that someone wanted to get rid of her like yesterday's trash. The analogy made her head snap up. The site where Ardie was allegedly injured had been "cleaned" thoroughly. "The branch! What did you do with it?"

Fortunately, Maggie had just completed a call.

"Arrgh!" she groaned. "In all the drama we forgot about that. It's outside on the back veranda. At least I hope it's still there."

"Thankfully it's summer and we haven't had a fire in ages. Your fingerprints will already be all over the thing, so go ahead and bring it in here."

While Maggie did as she asked, Lyra found a newspaper and covered a portion of the table. If the wood was where Maggie left it, the sheriff would need to see it.

"Yes!" Maggie yelled from out the back door and the next minute came down the hall with a grin, and carefully lay the branch on the paper.

Lyra's imagination ran riot. Without the flowers, it looked more sinister than something decorative. They both crouched and leaned over it, scouring every inch.

"I can't see anything. Although, since I found it on the bank near the farmhouse, it was probably immersed in water when the level of the stream rose overnight."

"Meaning there's no hope of any evidence." Lyra pursed her lips. "Still, we're no experts, and Walker might be able to do better than us by knowing exactly what to look for."

"I assume you mean blood or other bodily fluids."

Lyra grimaced, mimicking Maggie. "When you put it like that, perhaps we should be grateful it doesn't."

The front door suddenly burst open. Maggie grabbed at Lyra, and they sagged in relief at the sight of Patricia, who raced across the room and hugged them. "Thank goodness you're both okay."

"How did you know there'd been trouble?" Lyra mumbled into her neck.

"Carrie-Ann. She was out for a walk and heard the commotion at the end of the park and saw them bring Raylene out of her house on a stretcher. She came right back to the diner to tell me that you and Maggie were there. When you didn't return for ages, I called the station and Janie said you'd never been there. You've no idea what I've been thinking!" She took a steadying breath. "Now, what happened to Raylene?"

"Sorry, Mom, the sheriff asked us not to say, and since we got back, Maggie and I remembered something and need to speak to him again. I promise, it's urgent."

"Well, I have no idea where he is and neither did Janie, and where's the sense in running around looking for him with a murderer out there?" Patricia fumed for a moment, then shrugged. "He'll want your statements at some stage, and he knows where to find you."

Lyra could see that her mom was scared, but didn't like the idea of waiting for however long it took for Walker to be free to talk to her. "He's probably at the hospital in Destiny with Raylene, waiting to question her. Or he could be searching her home and the area around it. I guess we better leave him a message."

"I'll phone him." Maggie moved away to make the call.

Lyra offered to make fresh coffee, but Patricia's patience had worn thin.

"I don't care what Walker said about this being kept quiet. You are my daughter and I need you to tell me right now, young lady, why Carrie-Anne saw you covered in blood and obviously upset."

Thankful that she'd rinsed out the clothes before Patricia found them, Lyra capitulated a little. "Raylene is in a bad way, and that was her blood Carrie-Anne saw, but she's safe for the moment. Like you said, the murderer is still out there, and I'm afraid we've stirred up a hornet's nest."

Patricia's mouth gaped for a moment. "How?"

"We barely got to Raylene before she died," Lyra said flatly.

The door banged on its hinges, eliciting squeals from all three women and a bark from Cinnamon. *Doesn't anyone know how to enter a room a little less hastily?* Dan raced to Maggie, who'd finished with the phone. He took her chin and looked her over from head to toe. "Are you sure you're okay?"

Maggie shrugged at Lyra. "Sorry, I called him when I couldn't get the sheriff. I figured a bit of muscle might make us feel safer."

Dan's face was a shade of red that Lyra had never seen on him. The man was furious, and oddly his anger was directed at Maggie.

"You had no right to go there on your own and put yourself in danger."

Eyes narrowed; she removed his hand none too gently. "Ah, excuse me. I was with Lyra and Cinnamon. And what do you mean by no right?"

Dan's angry face was a little scary, but Maggie topped it with ease, and her quieter voice dripped shards of ice as she stood rigidly in front of him.

All that color drained from Dan in a couple of heartbeats. "That didn't come out right. I just meant, I was so worried about you and wish I'd been there to protect you."

"That's all very sweet, but you never get to tell me what I can or can't do." The ice was still evident, with perhaps a little thawing around the edges.

"No, I wouldn't dream of it," Dan insisted.

"I believe you just did."

"I wasn't thinking clearly. All I could imagine since your call was you in the hands of the murderer, and my brain turned to mush. You know how I feel about you. If I somehow lost you, I don't know how I'd get over it."

Lyra had to admire his backtracking and got a little mushy inside at the way he looked deep into Maggie's eyes as if she were a precious jewel. Apparently, she wasn't the only one who thought so.

Mom sighed while Maggie's anger slipped from her like melted ice cream.

She took a step closer to him. "I'm not sure I do know how you feel, but don't do it again."

Dan grabbed Maggie to his chest and kissed her hard. Lyra's hand went to her throat, and sounds she hadn't known she was capable of bubbled out of her. It had to be the most romantic fight she'd ever witnessed.

Arabelle, who had apparently snuck in after Dan, coughed and looked away for a second, but it was hard not to watch.

Patricia clapped her hands. "I guess this means they are officially boyfriend and girlfriend. Not that there was any doubt to the rest of us, but I was wondering how many more years they could drag it out for before they admitted it to themselves."

The room erupted with laughter, and Lyra noticed her cheeks were damp. Maggie and Dan had been sweet on each other for so long and finally they'd come out about it—intentionally or not.

When Dan let her go, Maggie's eyes shone, and she seemed breathless. No surprises there.

"As much as I'm delighted by this romantic interlude, I must find Walker," Lyra said quietly to Patricia.

"Of course, dear." Mom nodded, happily lost in the moment, and obviously not listening.

Lyra sighed. "Listen, everyone. I have evidence that the sheriff needs. Have any of you seen him?"

There was much shaking of heads and Maggie tapped her forehead. "I don't know how something so urgent keeps slipping my mind."

"Oh, I think we appreciate how it could happen," Patricia chuckled.

Maggie blushed. "Let's go find him, Lyra."

"Wherever you're going, I'm going, and no arguments. Please," Dan added somewhat helplessly.

"Fine. Does anyone know where the sheriff would be? Last time we saw him, he was going to the hospital, and now he's not answering his phone."

"He could be anywhere," Arabelle stated. "After listening to Carrie-Anne, my advice is to leave him another message and stay off the streets."

"If you won't listen to me, then at least listen to Arabelle. Like you said, whoever hurt Raylene will know soon enough, if they don't already, that she's alive. There's no point in inviting early retribution even if Dan is glued to your sides until the sheriff gets back to you."

Naturally, Patricia was concerned, but Lyra found it increasingly difficult to leave it to hope that Walker would check his message anytime soon. It occurred to her that the deputy hadn't been where he was supposed to be at Raylene's, and this made her worry for Walker's safety too. To appease Patricia, she did leave yet another message on his phone, and also called his office and spoke with Janie again.

Patricia watched her the entire time, and when she was done, nodded toward the back veranda.

"What's on your mind?" Lyra asked as soon as they were outside.

"I was about to ask you the same thing. Obviously we all know about Raylene and the murder, but I can tell you know more than you're sharing. I also know that you like to keep things close to your chest for a variety of reason including protecting me, but I think I deserve to know as much as possible while we have the time to do so."

Lyra looked across the backyard and the stream, wondering if they were being watched right now. She wrapped her arms across her chest. "The thing is, I'm not sure if what I think happened is fact or just guesswork. The longer we wait, the less certain I am, but it could be incredibly important if it is right."

Patricia walked back and forth across the veranda before stopping beside her. "As much as I hate your involvement in any way, I'd be lying if I didn't say you were good at sifting through clues and putting them together in a different way. I trust your instincts to do what you must." She blinked a couple of times and took in a deep breath. "Only, please be careful."

The 360 turn was a shock, and it took a few seconds before Lyra could react. "Thanks, Mom. It's never my intention to stress you out or worry you. I know that sometimes I get so caught up I can't see beyond making things right."

"That's what makes you a great chef. I just hope that after you find the sheriff and get this off your chest, you can let it go."

Lyra aimed for positivity and fell a little short. "I'll definitely try."

Until the murderer was caught, she couldn't imagine not worrying for them all.

25

Walker chose that moment to appear from around the side of the house. "Does she ever listen to you, Mrs. St. Claire?"

Patricia shrugged. "Not as often as I'd like these days, but she has always had a mind of her own."

"Hmmm. Okay, where is it?"

Desperately needing to know if the branch was a missing piece of the puzzle, Lyra led the way inside where she pointed at the table. The others backed away to allow the sheriff plenty of room.

Giving the group a curious glance, he pulled on gloves and took a pair of tweezers from his shirt pocket. "Just because the time frame works out, there is no way we can assume this is connected to Ardie's murderer."

They nodded in unison, though they weren't all aware that this was what Walker had been called to see.

"As long as we all understand that. Now, who has touched the wood since you found it?"

"We can't be sure on the day of the party, but Maggie found and decorated the branch. Today, only she touched it," Lyra told him evenly.

He stared into the distance for a moment, and Lyra wondered if he was taking notes in his head the way she did.

"Have you heard how Raylene is?" she dared to ask.

His eyes refocused. "She's not out of the woods but is doing okay."

"Do you think she's safe in the hospital?" Patricia asked.

"There's an officer on duty, and there will be around the clock." He gritted his teeth. "Could I have a little quiet please?"

Dutifully, they stayed silent as he scoured the wood. The tweezers lifted and hovered at the very edge of it for a few seconds until they closed over something Lyra couldn't make out.

"You found something?" she blurted.

He pulled the almost invisible strand off the wood and lifted it to his face. "A hair."

"Wow," Maggie exclaimed. "I hope it's not mine."

He turned his head and frowned before dropping the hair into a plastic bag. After another sweep, he stood back and nodded. "The hair could belong to anyone who has been near the stream, but it's still a good find and just a pity you didn't remember about it earlier."

Lyra tensed at the censure, although she did agree. "There was no way of knowing that a branch on our side of the stream might be from the crime scene. It only occurred to us after Raylene showed us where Ardie supposedly fell and the fact that there was nothing he could have hurt himself on unless it had been moved."

"It was actually a brilliant supposition from Lyra that brought it all together," Maggie told him proudly.

"Hmmm. I'm taking the branch with me so I can get it tested for other DNA. Does anyone have anything else to add or something they've forgotten about?"

The group looked at each other.

"I'm sure there isn't anything else," Lyra said guiltily.

"Are Maddie and Lyra safe here?" Dan demanded.

Walker shuffled his feet. "I am a bit thin on officers. Perhaps you should stay here for a night or two. Would that be all right?"

"There are three of us living here," Maggie reminded the men. "We're hardly helpless."

Patricia sniffed. "Dear girl, you may be capable of scaring off a killer with a snarky comment, but I prefer to have a strong man around to increase the odds-on safety."

Dan unwisely snorted, and Maggie glared at him, but he kept his eyes averted.

"If it will make you feel better, then I'd love to stay."

"By all means, do it just for me." Patricia chuckled and headed to the kitchen. Fear had apparently given way to a touch of mischievousness.

With that settled, Lyra walked the sheriff to the driveway, a little miffed that no one had checked what she thought about it. "I hope you find something that will point to the killer. Maybe fingerprints on the knife?"

He shook his head at her attempt to find out more. "That would help, but the knife was wiped clean, or gloves were used. Meanwhile, I have a lot of people to interview, so please stay out of trouble. It would be nice to have one less person to worry about."

A warm glow annoyed her. She shouldn't read anything into a throwaway comment like that, but she gulped anyway. "I'd like to visit Raylene tomorrow."

"That should be all right. There will be a guard at her door, so I'll send word that you'll be showing up and to let you in."

"Oh yes, what happened to the guard at the house?"

He leaned in closer, his breath tickling her cheek. "We found him locked in a neighbor's shed. He was unconscious from a blow to the back of his head."

She gasped. "Like Ardie?"

He stared into her eyes so close to his. "Just like that. I'm going to do everything in my power to keep you all safe, but you must do your part. If you're going to the hospital tomorrow, take someone with you."

Her cheeks were burning, and she couldn't look away. "I promise to be extra careful, and I am sorry we didn't connect the crime with the branch."

"I'm sorry too. I shouldn't have come down on you so hard. I guess I expect too much. What can I say? I may have one or two flaws."

She swayed theatrically and grabbed the nearest post. "You?"

His mouth twitched. "Cut the sarcasm, Chef."

Diverting the heat by teasing him helped. "But you're never wrong."

"Fine. Have your fun. I probably deserve it."

"Probably?"

"I'm going before you completely damage my self-confidence."

"I think you'll survive."

He grinned and shuffled his feet a little as if he wanted to add something more. Instead, he touched his brim and went down the drive to where his car was parked. The light came on as he got in, and she saw him pick up his phone and clip it on the dash before he drove away.

It was funny how he came into her thoughts more readily these days. Although, this could have a lot to do with the fact that they were in close contact because of the crimes.

Interrupting her musing, Cinnamon, who had been oddly absent since before Walker arrived, came running from the closed diner with a piece of paper in her mouth which she dropped at Lyra's feet.

"What have you got there, girl?"

The beagle growled and looked back at the diner.

Lyra scooped up the wrinkled page and flattened it out a little, stepping into the light of the veranda. *"Celebrity Chef loses another employee after attempted suicide is thwarted the first time, but unfortunately not the second."*

Lyra gasped at the headline and this time really did need the security of something to lean on. Cinnamon whined a little.

"Where did you get this?"

The beagle took several paces toward the diner, growling once more.

"Someone gave this to you to bring to me?"

A soft woof agreed with her.

Cinnamon didn't look hurt, so that was a relief, but what did this mean? The killer was clearly taunting her, because if this had been in the paper, she would have known about it. Local or international ones wouldn't matter in this instance, because well-meaning friends would bring it to her attention—not to mention those who didn't have her best interests at heart. Plus, it hadn't happened yet.

A trickle of sweat ran down her back. Assuming that it was a taunt of what was to come, her beagle would have made more of a fuss if the person who gave this to Cinnamon was still at the diner, but that didn't mean he wasn't nearby. What if he'd been waiting for the sheriff to leave before taking his next step? Which led to two more questions.

Was it one man or more?

Who did they want to hurt most—Raylene or Lyra?

Obviously whoever it was had a vendetta against Lyra for something other than thwarting their attempts to get some dirt on her. But they also wanted Raylene out of the picture because—she knew too much—about them?

Lyra pulled out her phone and called Walker. Typically, it went to voice mail. If she called the station, what would she say? A bogus one-liner on a piece of paper was hardly proof of anything, and with Walker and his deputies around town and who knew where else, Janie would be the only one manning the station. No, it would be better to keep trying the sheriff, so she was on her own for now.

Cinnamon whined again, and Lyra knelt to hug her. "I'll find out what they're up to, but you have to stay here."

"And where might you be going?" Arms on her hips, Maggie leaned against the farmhouse doorframe.

Lyra thrust the paper at her. She trusted this woman with her life.

Maggie frowned. "What the heck? Does this mean that they're going to try again to kill Raylene?"

"Lower your voice," Lyra hissed. "I think that's exactly what it means. Walker's out somewhere else, so I must go to the hospital."

"They won't let you in."

"Walker said he would leave my name at the door for tomorrow, but if he hasn't done that yet, then I'll just wait and keep an eye on anyone coming or going."

"If they already left, they'll be there ahead of you."

"And they'll have the same issue of getting in."

Maggie frowned. "I don't suppose I can talk you out of this?"

"Sorry, I feel really strongly that I need to be there."

"Okay, but I'm coming too."

"Are you sure?"

"Hah! You should know by now that some things will never change."

Ever since they'd begun working together, Maggie had always stuck by her. Even when that wasn't a particularly good idea.

Dan stepped into the light with a resigned expression and the car keys. The only reason he didn't argue was because she knew that once her mind was made up, Maggie was as stubborn as Lyra. And naturally, where Maggie went, if danger was involved, Dan would have to be there too.

26

Leaving Cinnamon, her self-appointed bodyguard, had been hard, but since she would never be allowed into the hospital, it was pointless to take her, then lock the poor beagle up in the car for who knew how long.

The drive to the hospital seemed longer than usual. Long enough to agonize over upsetting Patricia and Arabelle, who were all fired up again knowing that this time Lyra wasn't waiting for the sheriff. She'd shown them the note, which gave them pause, but it was only Dan's assurance that he would accompany them that allowed the older women to let them leave the house.

Lyra parked away from the main entrance and avoided the lamps and other cars. The three of them studied the area in front of them and behind.

"There are two security guards outside and possibly more inside." Maggie pointed out the obvious. "You can't get in."

"Assuming they belong to Walker, I should be able to persuade them."

That made Maggie grip the dash as she leaned forward to peer through the glass. "What makes you think they aren't the murderer's men?"

Lyra tapped the steering wheel. "They're wearing uniforms, and the insignia looks like a security firm I've heard of."

"Do you think that's proof enough?" Dan asked.

"No," she admitted glumly. "Why wouldn't Walker have his deputies here instead of security guards?"

"They could work for the hospital. It's normal to have security guards these days, and the sheriff did say he was short-staffed," he reminded her.

"True, but there's two of them guarding one door, and I've never seen any around Destiny that look like they do, have you?" While being fit wasn't a crime, the security guards she'd seen lately were a lot older and didn't have arms that bulged the way these two did.

Maggie peered through the windscreen. "Hmm. I see what you mean. They must work out—a lot. And now that you've put the idea in my head, they do look kinda mean. What do want to do?"

"Well, we can't reach Raylene from here." Lyra made to get out of the car, but Maggie didn't move a muscle. "If you're too scared, you can wait in the car. It's not like they're going to attack me for talking to them." At least she hoped they wouldn't.

Maggie nodded. "Naturally I'm scared, but actually I think it would be best if I tried to reach someone who has some answers and a way of finding out where Walker is. Plus, I can get help in the likely chance that you get into trouble." While she said this matter-of-factly, her voice shook.

"You're right. I'll try to get inside, but after that I have no plan except to locate Raylene. I'll stay with her and call to let you know she's okay."

"What about me? The sheriff would be furious if I let you go in there on your own."

"Fine, but try not to look so threatening and don't say anything."

Dan nodded yet made no promises.

"And if I get hold of anyone, I'll message you," Maggie said firmly.

They stared at each other for a second or two.

"Stay safe," the women said at the same time and smiled.

Dan and Lyra left the car and made their way to where the two staunch security guards watched their approach. The one on the far side of the door muttered something from the shadows and disappeared around the side of the building. Before she could say anything, the other one pointed to the sign on his left.

"Visiting hours are over."

Lyra drew herself up to her average height. "I'm not visiting. I have reason to believe that a patient is in danger, and I must ensure she is safe."

He glanced at Dan, palm caressing the gun on his hip. "You'll appreciate that people try to get inside all the time. Why is this person in danger? And from whom?" He glanced to his left and right.

"I'm not sure who wants to hurt her, but it could be the person who tried to kill her earlier today and put her in this hospital."

His eyes narrowed. "Do you have a name?"

"Raylene Dwyer."

The guard nodded impassively and pulled out a walkie-talkie, a more upmarket model than the ones they'd used on the sets of Lyra's shows, and she'd had the best.

"Wait here, and I'll see if I can help." He moved away a little to speak quietly into the handset.

This gave her a slight hope that they were on the level, since he couldn't possibly know every patient, but the police would have explained the situation. Unless…

"You obviously know about her, right?" she asked when he snapped the handset back in the holder located on his shoulder.

His eyes narrowed. "I can't divulge any information, and you should leave."

Lyra grabbed Dan's arm as he took a step forward. "Believe me, we understand the need for security, but could you just nod or shake your head to this one question? Is Sheriff Walker from Fairview already here, or is he still on his way?"

Maybe he was good at his job, and physical stuff, but right now the guard looked more like an overgrown schoolboy, confused by a math problem which wasn't adding up the way it was supposed to, and then he simply looked worried.

"He's also a close friend of mine, and he'll want to know what I have to tell him right away," she pressed. It wasn't exactly a lie because Walker would want her news. She just wasn't sure what kind of friend he currently was (close was a gross misrepresentation) or how happy he'd be to see her tonight. "It's about the case and incredibly important."

"I can't let you in, but why don't you call him?"

"I have, repeatedly. He's not picking up." She held out her phone to him. "See, that's his number."

Oddly the guard's eyes lit up as if he had an epiphany. "That doesn't prove much, but I guess it won't hurt to say that he's on site and doesn't want to be disturbed right now. He said he had too much to do, and he'll come see you at the farmhouse when he's done."

Step one achieved. Now she knew that this wasn't Walker's man. Okay, she wasn't 100 percent sure, but unless he'd given Walker a description of her, she hadn't told him her name, so how did the guard know who she was and where she lived? "Thank you for letting me know. I think it best that I speak to him face-to-face, so please tell him when you can that I'll wait here until he's done; that would be awesome."

This time he shook his head firmly. "I can't let you wait out here. It might be dangerous. Why don't you tell me what information you have, and I'll pass it on?"

"That's so nice of you to be worried. If you let me in, I'll find him myself and save you any more bother."

Arms crossed, eyes narrowed again, he snorted. "It's more than my job's worth. How do I know you're not the person he's looking for?"

"Because I'm a woman, and the attempted murderer is a man according to the victim."

He smirked a little. "You could be in league with him, or this could be the guy with you."

The guard was completely right, but that didn't stop her frustration scaling new heights, especially when his mouth tightened into a firm line. "I can assure you I'm not." Lyra sighed and moved several feet away from the door to try Walker's number again while Dan paced back and forth like a caged lion. When it went to voice mail, she did leave a message. It was all she could come up with, but was it enough?

Time was ticking away, and maybe Raylene didn't have much left. The man who instigated this was extremely dangerous. Taunts or not, she believed him when he said this wasn't over. For all she knew, he or one of his men was inside already.

With that on her mind, there was no way she could simply head back to Fairview. Somehow, she had to get to Raylene and make sure she was okay. Walker too, if he were really here.

Between the main entrance and the parking lot was a lush, grassed area. A large tree stood in the middle, with a wooden bench underneath facing the front door. It was a good vantage point to watch every move the guards made and make sure no one else entered.

The evening was warm, with a gentle breeze that at any other time would be perfect. Instead, her skin prickled, and she had a slight headache from trawling through scenarios in her mind. From here she could barely make out Maggie, who had slid down in the passenger seat. A tiny amount of light reflected off the rear mirror, and Lyra guessed Maggie was still making calls.

The guard checked on her every couple of minutes and twice spoke into the walkie-talkie attached to the shoulder of his uniform. After half an hour, when the possibilities of what was going on inside drove her to the verge of begging him to let her in, the other guard came back. They conferred for a while, looking in her direction, then both hurried inside.

While it made her nervous why they'd left their posts, it might be her only chance to get inside. "This is it," she whispered urgently, and raced to the sliding doors which opened immediately with Dan hot on her heels. Slipping quietly inside, Lyra noted the reception area had a counter which the nurses sat behind, thankfully too busy working on computers to notice her. Scooting by to reach the stairwell, she wondered fleetingly if this was too easy. Where had the guards gone? There was no time to waste valuable seconds pondering this. The sooner she got to the ward and found Raylene, the better.

She knew from when Leroy was here that the wards for less serious injuries were on the third floor, and that's where she headed, taking the steps two at a time. Of course, Raylene could be in the emergency department, but Walker said she was doing okay, which implied she'd be in a ward by now.

A little out of breath, she turned to Dan. "I have this feeling we don't have much time. Will you take Ward B, and I'll take this one?"

He hesitated for a minute, but finally nodded. "You better be careful," he told her before racing across the hallway and disappearing through the door.

Taking a big breath, she pushed open the fire door to Ward A, wincing as it creaked a little. Poking her head around it, she peered down the corridor, which was empty. Several doors on either side meant risking disturbing any patients in them, but she had to take the chance.

The doorway on the right was the nurse's station. It was wide with a long counter. Beeps from several screens cut through the silence along with murmurings. Two nurses sat facing each other by the far wall. They sipped from mugs, discussing their children.

Lyra crouched as low as she could and scuttled by. The first door on the left opened quietly. Inside a man lay curled under the covers, snoring gently. The next room held a woman who faced the windows. Her hair was streaked with gray, so definitely not Raylene.

Back to the right, Lyra's fingers reached the handle just as she caught a muffled cry and looked around for something to use as a weapon. The place was so clean and tidy that there wasn't even a stray bit of machinery left idle in the hall. Hopefully Walker would check his phone very soon. Maggie would say it was stupid to act so recklessly, yet how could she walk away and not help Raylene if it was possible?

She did take one more precaution before turning the handle as gently as possible, then opened the door with no idea what or who she would encounter. Taking a deep breath, she peeked inside—and gasped!

27

A guard stood over what she assumed was Raylene. It was hard to tell since he held a pillow over her face while the woman's arms and legs thrashed about.

"Get off her!" Lyra yelled, simultaneously pressing the button on her phone, having pre-dialed the police emergency number.

The guard spun—Roman Harper! Lyra recognized his face from the research she'd done. With the pressure relaxed, Raylene managed to push the pillow from her face; her wrists were heavily bandaged, reminding Lyra of why she was here. Judging by the beet red of her checks and the paleness of her lips, Lyra was just in time. And the only reason the pillow stayed off was due to Roman drawing his gun. Even if the police reacted as fast as humanly possible to Lyra's call, it was doubtful that she and Raylene could be saved from a bullet.

"Come over here." He waved the gun to the bed. Raylene had scooted up and cowered by the headboard. Lyra went to her side and took a trembling hand.

"How touching." He sneered, throwing a set of handcuffs at her. "Put them on."

A feeble attempt at catching allowed the cuffs to hit the floor with a clatter. Three pairs of eyes darted to the door.

Several heartbeats later, he growled, "Try that again and you won't see outside this room again."

Awkwardly, she did as he asked. It meant Raylene could move freely, but as scared as she clearly was, how would that help them? "What are you going to do with us?"

With the back of his hand, he wiped a bead of sweat from his forehead. "Let me worry about that. If you hadn't interfered, and she'd done what she was supposed to, it wouldn't have come to this." The gun waved between them.

Lyra licked her dry lips. "Did you think I wouldn't try to protect myself and the people I love?"

"Do they love you, is a better question? Surely what you can offer financially is the only incentive for hanging around a has-been celebrity."

Lyra stiffened. "You wouldn't understand that people work with me because they enjoy it and they're loyal. Not everyone does things solely for money."

"Oh, really?" He smirked. "By now you know that Raylene was all about the money."

"That's not the truth. After you threatened her and sent Ardie to blackmail her, she could do nothing else but get the job with me."

He shrugged carelessly. "We all have choices."

"That's true. I want to live in Fairview without being hounded, and you want a big story. The problem for you is that there isn't one, and no one really cares that I live there."

"Are you kidding me?" He snorted. "What do you think this is all about?"

"It's about you and some vendetta you have for me. I admit to being curious as to what that is."

"How clever of you to work that out. Lucky for me, no one knows that except a nosey chef and a woman who can't do anything right. One won't be missed, and the other will always be at the center of a murder inquiry—maybe more than one. After all, you're always there when someone dies, right?"

"You intend to frame me? I can't see how, considering I don't know Ardie and it was me who found the body." Even as she spoke, she could imagine the headlines he might manufacture. Her stomach churned, and Raylene, so pale and possibly on the verge of fainting, whimpered tragically.

"She needs water." In hindsight it was a stupid request when Roman had been in the process of killing her not so long ago.

"She needs to shut up."

The way he spat the words at her caused both knees to shake. Still, it seemed that she was doomed anyway, so if she could keep him talking, it meant there was always a slim chance that the police would get here in time—the real ones.

Roman walked around the room, looking in cupboards and drawers. The frown made it clear that he couldn't find whatever he was looking for. Probably something to kill them both, and just because there wasn't something here, didn't mean he couldn't locate it in another room. She had to stall him some more.

"If this is really all about money, I still have some. I could pay you to leave us alone."

"Don't you worry your pretty little head about that. Money is the least of my problems."

She didn't like the way he eyed Raylene and herself. "What if I double it? *And* give you a scoop as well as forget all about this episode?"

"Do you really think I'm that stupid?" he growled. "As soon as you got out there, your mouth would work overtime to bring me down."

"We're not all made that way."

He came across the room like a panther and poked her in the chest. "Look me in the eyes and tell me you wouldn't tell your sheriff everything."

She gulped, not sure how good a liar she was under any circumstances, let alone being terrified. "If you promised not to harm Raylene, I would give you time to get away."

"As tempting as that is, I think I'll pass," he scoffed, patting her cheek in a condescending way that smarted in both senses.

Her eyes watered just as her phone buzzed.

"I'll have that." He snatched it from her back pocket.

Her heart dropped at losing the only lifeline she possessed. They really were alone in this. It was a shame that Raylene wasn't hooked up to a machine that they could buzz for help. Hang on. Where was the usual buzzer? Raylene was still curled up at the head of the bed, and Lyra couldn't see the lead, so it must be around the other side of it.

Okay, reaching that wasn't going to happen from here. What else could she do or try? And who was messaging her? Was Walker here yet? Or had Roman already dealt with the sheriff? That idea made her nauseous, and she took a half step toward the window. *Please let him be safe.*

"What the heck are you up to?" Roman waved the gun at her to back away from the glass.

"I'm going to sit on the bed with Raylene. Is that okay? My legs are a bit jelly-like."

"Sure. Take a load off, your highness." He grabbed the handcuffs and yanked her to him. "On second thoughts, I need to get something, and you're going to help me."

"W-w-what do you need?"

He pulled her in front of him, ignoring the question. "Move to the door. Now." Putting the gun to her back and pressing it painfully into her ribs, he hissed over his shoulder, "You better not leave that bed. You hear me?"

She saw Raylene's head bob about like the dog on a car dashboard, then he pushed Lyra into the hall. She stumbled, but he held on so tight she had no chance to fall, forcing her to walk close to the wall. Lyra imagined this was so they'd be out of the line of the security cameras. As soon as they reached the next door, he bundled her into that room.

A man lifted his head from the pillow but slumped back. Obviously, he was drugged up, and Lyra was glad about one less person being hurt.

Roman checked out the drugs hanging from the pole, then yanked the drip from the man's arm. "This will do nicely," he gloated, taking no heed of the moan from the bed.

Lyra gasped. "You can't use that on us. You don't know what's in it or what the patient has."

"What does it matter?"

That was the first time Lyra could recall that she didn't think what a lovely sight twinkling eyes were.

He was a sadist and really did intend to kill them. It must have been self-preservation, thinking that she stood a chance of talking him out of it or bribing him to walk away. The look on his face when he held that pillow over Raylene's head proved he had no room for mercy or a change of heart.

Death was the means to an end, and he was fixated solely on that endgame without thought or care for anyone or anything else. Despite having known people like this in her past, it still horrified her and at the same time made her sad.

Footsteps in the hall were enough for him to drop the IV tube and needle to the floor and plant the gun back under her ribs. She would have some serious bruising—if she got out of this alive.

Voices, only slightly muffled, came through the closed door. "Mrs. Lamont needs more antibiotics, then I'll check on Ms. Dwyer to see if she needs more sedation." The person sighed. "The last time I checked on her, it was difficult to get away. The poor woman is traumatized and doesn't want to be alone. I guess her guard is in with her. Can you handle the drug round for the rest of the ward?"

"No problem. See you back at the station."

Footsteps retreated, and the door opened wider. Roman pulled her behind him just as the nurse entered. Only, it wasn't a nurse. Walker dove into the room and did an impressive roll across the floor to come up on his feet facing them, gun in hand. Lyra took the opportunity of a loosening grip on her arm to drop to her knees.

"Give it up. Or I will shoot."

"Oh, I don't think you will, Sheriff. I hear you quite like the chef."

The gun touched her temple. Again, none too gently.

"Let her go," Walker commanded. "Murder carries tough penalties, and you don't want to make things worse."

"Worse," Roman scoffed. "Are you kidding me right now? How could things be any worse?"

Walker raised an eyebrow. "Obviously I can't see you getting a light sentence, but it will be lighter without another two or three deaths added to the count."

The gun wavered, but Lyra had no doubts Roman would make good his threat. With her heart threatening to burst from her chest, she remained still, knowing that if he did shoot her, Raylene would be safe along with the poor woman in the bed, because Walker would do his job. It was a darn shame they hadn't gotten the chance to find out if there could be something between them.

Stressful situations had a habit of making her mind wander, and bizarrely this helped to keep her calm, so she let it continue. Roman hated Lyra. This was crystal clear. There had to be a reason, and now that he had no scoop, if that had ever been his intention, he wanted her dead. Somehow at some time she had done or said something to bring this down on not only her but Raylene and others she cared about. That made it her job to fix this, and she wouldn't risk one more life.

"You should kill me and get it over with."

28

"Lyra!" Walker yelled at her. "Don't say that!"

She raised her chin and looked him in the eyes. "I'm sorry, but I really think it's for the best. I'm the person he really wants to hurt. Poor Raylene was simply a means to get to me. If I'm gone, it's all over and you can arrest or shoot him—it's a no-brainer."

"Would you shut up!"

Walker had never yelled at her with quite so much feeling, and it would be almost touching if he wasn't so furious. "Do you have a better solution? Because this guy doesn't."

"This guy?" the killer raged. "You have no idea who I am, do you?"

Lyra shrugged. "You're the man who thinks it's okay to kill people to right some perceived wrong."

"Perceived?" he hissed. "You're so privileged you can't see the people around you and what you do to them. You've ruined countless lives because you're spoiled and rich."

"And you have no idea what you're talking about. I studied and worked hard to get where I am."

"Maybe that was true at the beginning, until you started stepping on people to get to the top."

Lyra flinched. Her world in LA crumbled several months back, and bad things had happened. This guy knew all about her, and since he didn't wanted money from her, this had never been about extortion. He wanted revenge, plain and simple, and she wasn't

225

about to die without knowing. "If I hurt anyone, I can assure you it was completely unintentional. Unfortunately, I had an agent who didn't care about other people. I allowed him to make bad decisions, but he is paying for what he did."

"Excuses! People with money have all the excuses under the sun and take none of the responsibility for their actions. I don't care about your greedy agent."

He was so close she saw the flecks in his eyes. A memory jarred her. These eyes reminded her of a man who'd tried to hurt her. A man who was in jail at this very moment. "You sound and look an awful lot like Cameron Willetts. Any relation?"

He laughed maniacally. "The penny's dropped at last. I heard you were making inquiries. Well, at this stage it doesn't really matter that you know I'm his father. Luckily, Cameron wanted to make it on his own, and changed his name to his mother's maiden years before he entered your competition."

She chewed the inside of her cheek to stem a new fear. Confirming his name meant once he killed her, he'd have to kill Finn if he wanted to get away. And Raylene. They needed time. Time for him to make a mistake and for Finn to get the upper hand somehow. Time to think of another plan.

"Make his own way? He cheated and killed to win the first competition. Did Cameron put you up to this? I'm not sure how he could from prison."

"We all do what we must, and he didn't have to do a thing from prison. I do what I want when I want, and since he can't do anything about it right now, this is the only job I have." He spat out the words followed by a maniacal laugh. "You know, it didn't have to be murder, even though what you did to Cameron warrants it. If you and that stupid reporter had played the game, you would have been ruined, but alive. That's all I needed as payment for destroying my son's life."

His eyes were now feverish, and beads of sweat dotted his face. Walker nodded imperceptibly. Did he want her to continue? She had to assume it was to waste time until the police arrived.

"Don't you mean ruin me for a second time? Your son used me to win a competition he couldn't on his own, and because of the scandal I lost my show and other engagements. All that aside, Raylene did nothing to wind up being your pawn. At least let her go."

"No one here is innocent." He sneered. "Your waitress was happy taking my money when it suited her."

Lyra shook her head, making the gun smack against her temple again—it wasn't an experience a person could get used to. "Like I said, she felt she had no choice after being threatened, but she changed her mind, which any reasonable person would do once they saw how far you were prepared to go."

"You're right, she did want out, but it was too late." His eyes narrowed as he studied Walker, who hadn't moved.

Or had he? Something about the way he stood looked awkward. Lyra needed to get Roman's focus back on her. "It's never too late to change. I'm sure your son wouldn't want you to go to prison or die because of him."

"What do you know about my son? He could have been famous, but you let him down when he asked for help."

"Is that what he told you?" Lyra's horror battled with her common sense and won. "He stalked me and hurt people to get what he wanted. I could hardly reward him for it by giving him a dead man's prize he never earned."

"Lies. All lies. He had great potential and should have won any of your ridiculous contests. Instead, he's in jail for the best years of his life. We could have worked side-by-side, pandering to the rich and famous like you did, until he was mature enough to take over my empire."

"I hear your empire is crumbling. Is that why you needed a famous son? To get back what you squandered with your tacky articles? The problem with your plan is that Cameron couldn't have handled the pressure and fame. He needed guidance. What did you do to help him?"

Judging by the apoplectic face above her, she had scored a direct hit.

"I was waiting until he proved himself. The boy was weak and needed tough love," he blustered. "I saw how he grew in confidence on your show and how much he improved in a short time."

"You mean, my ridiculous show? Yes, he did gain confidence, and then he killed someone."

"Like I said. That was your fault. He got desperate to prove himself the best when you wouldn't accept it."

All this time Lyra had been waiting for Finn to make some sign, and with his finger pointed to her left, she had it. "I have the feeling that you're the one he wanted to prove himself to, but I doubt you'll admit that, which means we're back where we started. You're going to kill me, so do it already."

Roman stiffened, and with every ounce of strength, Lyra elbowed him in the solar plexus and flung herself to the left.

Walker sprung through the air, grabbing for the gun. At the same time another body hurtled from the room opposite and tackled Roman around the knees. They landed heavily, and the gun dropped to the floor a few feet away. Lyra quickly kicked it out into the hall.

Kaden had Roman pinned, and Walker pulled out his cuffs and yanked the criminal's hands behind his back to clip them on him.

"Is it really over?" Lyra was shaking uncontrollably, and Kaden climbed from the killer and pulled her to him.

"Shhh. You're safe now."

"H-h-how did you know to come here tonight?"

"Maggie. She couldn't reach the sheriff and was scared you were in over your head."

"Which you were," Walker growled.

"I got another note like the other articles he had printed, threatening Raylene. I couldn't reach you, and I was worried about you both," Lyra explained.

"There was absolutely no need to endanger yourself. I had a feeling there was going to be another attempt on Raylene tonight, so I made noises that I had somewhere else to be and made my way here by a back road. It wasn't intended to give you permission to go off on one of your sleuthing escapades."

Roman struggled in the cuffs and swore, something about women who didn't know their place. Walker told him to be quiet and the man continued to glare at her.

Knowing he was right, yet not done with her self-appointed task, she hurried out the door. Happy to get away from another member of the Willetts family. "We should check on Raylene," she called over her shoulder. The door was locked, which was worrying. "Raylene? It's me—Lyra. Can you open up?"

Inside, something metal scraped across the floor, and the door opened to reveal Maggie. "Am I glad to see you safe. Kaden made us wait here." Maggie hugged Lyra, then sat on the bed beside the pale woman and put her arms around her. "Raylene's been very brave and told me what you'd done. You saved her life, Lyra. Twice."

"Another few seconds, and I would have suffocated," Raylene croaked. "You're a hero."

Roman growled from the doorway, and Walker pulled hard on the handcuffs. "I'll be back once I hand him over to another officer."

Lyra rubbed her sore arms. "That reminds me. Those two security guards out front weren't for real, were they?"

Dan appeared in the doorway. "They were heavies but weren't interested in murder, and I managed to convince them to give themselves up." He rubbed raw and bruised knuckles.

"Good work, Dan." Walker scratched his head. "I have no idea where my officer from this door is. He was stationed there when Raylene was admitted."

"He's in the room opposite," Kaden said casually. "Out cold and snoring like a sheep dog with a lump on his head."

Finn and Kaden shared a look which Lyra couldn't read, and suddenly she was so bone weary she couldn't be bothered to work out why. Everyone she cared about was safe, and as far as she knew, no one in the hospital was badly harmed.

It was a good outcome, no matter what Finn thought of her. Only, deep down, now that she thought of him as Finn more often than not, it did matter.

29

A day later, Lyra placed the tray of coffees on the table as Arabelle came in the door. The woman eyed the knitting ladies, gave them a tepid greeting, and followed Lyra to the counter, waiting impatiently while she served someone else.

"Aren't you joining the group?" Lyra asked.

"I've been thinking about it, but my plans may change," she said mysteriously. "Actually, that's why I'm here—to discuss those plans. Do you have a minute?"

Arabelle had been hanging around since well before the whole Raylene debacle, and today she seemed finally ready to get whatever was bugging her out in the open.

"This sounds intriguing. We're a little short-staffed, so I'm afraid it will have to be here."

Arabelle took a minute, possibly to decide if Lyra was teasing, then simply nodded. "As you said, without Raylene, you're a person down again. I'd like to apply for the job," she said, lowering her voice while managing to inject a level of firmness.

Caught by surprise, Lyra's tact deserted her. "You?"

"Don't look so shocked." Arabelle sniffed. "I'm a better cook than most around town and would take orders better than many due to my orderly mind. Plus, I'm quite capable of wiping down tables without getting dragged into gossip." She nodded over her shoulder at the knitting group, who were still discussing the latest events.

Lyra had no doubt that Arabelle would put the women in their place. She'd also been inside Arabelle's house and could attest to her organized as well as tidy way of life, but why bring this up now? Was it only to do with her being shorthanded? Because that didn't make sense. "If you wanted to work here, why didn't you apply for a job before I hired Raylene?"

Arabelle glanced toward the kitchen and lowered her voice further. "I've been bored for some time, but I didn't want to work alongside Vanessa right away in case she thought I was judging or competing with her. You're aware that she desperately needed the money, but for a bolshie woman, she has very low self-esteem."

Lyra bit back a smile. It was all true. Vanessa who, not so long ago, lorded it over her friends and anyone else she could, had changed dramatically since her daughter went to jail for manslaughter. It was also a very kind thing that Arabelle did, since she was the one who pushed Vanessa when she was so low into applying at the diner. However, Lyra still wasn't convinced there could be a happy outcome if they both worked here. "You were keeping an eye on her, though, weren't you? I mean you came to the diner every day, and that wasn't usual."

"Of course. Times change, and she was in a bad way when Poppy went to prison. Before then, if you want to know the truth. When her husband died, she was like a cake left out in the air. Working here is just what she needed, and it cheered her up no end to finally earn her own money and feel useful. Now, I'd be happy to do what Raylene did, or work part-time since down the track you'll most likely want some younger blood."

Lyra almost laughed. Arabelle's honesty was in a way refreshing, though it was a concern how the two friends might get along working together. They'd certainly had their moments of holding grudges, but Lyra had some plans of her own, and Arabelle might be the answer to them. The question was would it be worth dealing with the two opinionated women on a daily basis, and could she circumvent any issues before they boiled over? Maybe. That word could be full of promise or herald disaster.

"I know you appreciate straight answers like I do, so while I can't say I'm totally convinced this will be a long-term proposition, it would certainly be a blessing to have you here for the meantime. If you can cook, that's a massive bonus, but you must work well with everyone."

Arabelle rubbed her hands together as if it were a done deal. "I understand, and you won't be disappointed. I've discussed it with Vanessa, and I can start on Monday. I'll take the early shift."

Lyra raised an eyebrow. "Oh, I see. You two worked this out before talking to me."

The woman shrugged. "No point in mucking around when a person's mind is made up, and there's nothing standing in the way, is there? And surely you've noticed that Vanessa isn't a morning person."

"Unlike you?" Lyra managed with a straight face. "While you make perfect sense, there is one thing I'd like to point out—I am the boss."

"Of course." Arabelle sniffed. "I certainly wouldn't undermine you."

Had Lyra been conned once again? That remained to be seen, but once she figured out that Arabelle had a good heart, and her bark was way worse than her bite, she'd found that she truly liked the woman. Fingers crossed she wasn't making a huge mistake, because the truth was she'd made a few recently. It did play havoc with a person's ability to make quick decisions, and that annoyed her.

Still, it appeared she had a new staff member, and there was no time like the present to get that out in the open. "You'd better come out and meet the team officially. They'll likely be… surprised."

Arabelle's mouth twitched. "I'm counting on it."

Since she'd seen Arabelle give a thumbs-up to Vanessa, Lyra left the server to take care of the diner and led her new employee into the kitchen. As luck would have it, everyone was there. Even Dan, who stood talking with Maggie at the office door.

"Excuse me, everyone. Could I have your attention? Arabelle will be starting work here on Monday. She's taking over Raylene's job until she's better."

Earl looked shell-shocked, and Maggie gaped while Patricia shook her head slightly. Even Dan frowned so bad his eyes squinted.

Leroy came away from the grill and eyed Arabelle. "Temporary, is it?"

Arabelle stared right back. "We'll see."

The tension was palpable and totally reasonable given the circumstances. Both Vanessa and Arabelle were strong-willed and opinionated. While Vanessa was eager to please most of the time, it could end in tears with the two of them together, and her team knew that as well as she did. They were her main concern, so she laid it on the line. "We do need another server and cook. Arabelle could be both of those things, but it depends on everyone working well together. If it doesn't work out, then we'll rethink things." There was a rather pregnant pause.

"Well, you said it—we do need the help," Leroy said graciously.

Arabelle nodded and turned to Earl. "I'd like to make this work, so I'll try not to scare you or the customers. You could give me a sign if I come across too strong. How does that sound?"

He flushed and offered a weak smile. It wasn't his best work, but at least the terrified deer-in-headlights look was gone.

"Maggie, could you pull out some paperwork for Arabelle while she's here to save time on Monday?"

"Let's go into the office." Maggie's attempt at casualness was reasonably effective.

Lyra noticed Vanessa in the entranceway, chewing her bottom lip. Arabelle said that she'd cleared it with her. Maybe this wasn't true. Second guesses were a pain in the you-know-what when all she wanted was a break from any drama.

Then there was Dan, who fidgeted outside the office door, glancing in several times. *Now what?*

"Do you need something, Dan?"

He stilled. "Ah... I wonder, do you have any champagne?"

Lyra laughed. Dan drank a beer now and again, but she'd never even seen him touch wine. "Are you serious?"

He nodded. "I have good news that I want to share with everyone. At least I think it is."

Lyra smiled. "Perfect. We could all use some of that."

"It's not for now," he protested. "Can I get it later? I didn't want to bother you, but Maggie's busy."

He seemed nervous, and sweat had broken out on his brow.

Patricia wiped her hands on her apron. "I could have got it for you, dear. Do we have some, Lyra?"

"Maggie would know for sure, but let's not disturb her. I'll check."

Lyra went to the chiller and stepped inside. Their liquor license allowed for sale of beers, wines, and spirits, but champagne wasn't a big seller in Fairview. It was nice to have some on hand for any special celebrations, and luckily there were two bottles tucked behind the bulk of the wines she preferred. She pulled them out and handed them to Dan. "Here you go."

He grinned like a schoolboy and walked out with the bottles, straight into Maggie and Arabelle.

"Ooh, what are they for?" Maggie checked the labels. "Must be something big, because you are not a bubbly kind of guy."

He looked away. "Nothing. I mean of course it's for something, but it's a surprise."

Maggie snorted. "I hate surprises."

"You do?" He blinked several times. "Why?"

"In my opinion they're overrated."

"Maggie, don't spoil Dan's good fortune." Patricia tutted. "He wants to share it with us."

"Really. I'll just slip that large foot of mine out of my mouth. You go right ahead and surprise us then."

He backed away. "Not now."

"Oh, come on, don't be shy," Maggie teased. "I'm sure it's a fancy car that you have to work on, right?"

His lips pursed. "I'm not saying."

"Man, you can be so annoying."

"Me? Why can't you be a little less…" He threw his hands in the air and stalked across the kitchen.

"What did I say? I'm just yanking your chain," Maggie called after him. "Don't you want to share the news while we're all together?"

He stopped at the door, watched by the whole team. With a huge sigh, he straightened, turned, and strode back. "Fine, but don't complain later, because you are going to be sorry you insisted," he growled at her.

Leroy hurried out from behind the grill, and Earl jumped in front of Maggie.

"For crying out loud, I'm hardly going to hurt her, am I?"

Dan looked at them like they were crazy, which was confusing when he was the one acting weirdly.

"I wouldn't like to think so." Finn marched into the kitchen. "What's all the yelling about?"

Dan was now red-faced. "I don't believe this! Who called the police?"

"No one, yet," Finn warned.

"All right, everyone, can we just relax for a minute while Dan gets this off his chest?" Lyra told

238

the group apprehensively. Surely Dan wasn't leaving Fairview. He seemed anxious and annoyed about something. Champagne didn't seem to marry with those emotions. Unless…

"Well, I guess there's no getting out of here and doing things the way I'd planned, so don't you dare blame me down the track, Maggie Parker."

"You already said that," she huffed. "Blame you for what?"

Dan shook his head one last time. "Okay. Here goes."

30

Dan knelt and put his hand in his pocket. Still sweating, but with a shy and hopeful grin, he removed a small jewelry box from his shirt pocket and held it out to Maggie.

"I know you're incredibly talented and you love to have fun, and I'm just a simple garage owner who finds it hard to get where you're coming from, but will you marry me?"

For the first time that Lyra could remember, Maggie was struck for words, and this lasted several moments while everyone else waited with bated breath.

Then, true to form, Maggie managed to squeak a rude response. "Open it and let me have a look first."

He blushed and fumbled with the box as Maggie threw herself at him. "I'm joking! I don't care if it's the ring off a can of soda. Yes, I'll marry you." She kissed him hard, and he fell backward, pulling her on top of him, missing the corner of the table by mere inches.

The others stood in a circle and clapped while Cinnamon barked at the back door, annoyed at missing out on the fun.

"Sheesh," Dan said as they scrambled to their feet. "I wish you'd told me before about the can. It would have saved me a fortune—and a broken spine."

Before Maggie could make a retort, he opened the box and placed the ring on her finger. "No backs."

"It's gorgeous," she sighed. "Exactly what I would have picked."

"Thank goodness. I don't like it when you get violent."

Maggie snorted and kissed him again. This time much gentler—and a little longer.

Lyra sniffed and, glancing around at her family and friends, saw that most of them were in the same boat, including Leroy and Earl. And Finn? Well, he was avoiding her gaze.

"I'm so glad I came by today to check on you," Kaden said from behind her.

She laughed delightedly. "Me too. Any chance of a hug?"

"You bet."

"Maybe not." Finn's voice held a touch of steel as he put himself between them.

"What's gotten into you?" she asked, laughter dying in her throat.

"I'm pretty sure this guy doesn't have the right to touch you."

Was this some sick joke? "Don't be ridiculous." Lyra couldn't even summon a smile, because Finn looked as though he wanted to do Kaden an injury.

The sheriff's chin jutted at the chef. "Am I wrong in saying that you have a fiancée?"

Lyra blinked. It was the first she heard of it, and so unlike Kaden not to share any news. Especially something so huge. "Is this true?"

"It is, but I wanted you to hear it from me." Kaden glared at the sheriff. "In fact, it's another reason why I came today."

"Sure, it is," Finn sneered.

Lyra ignored the testosterone flying about. "Well, I can't pretend that I'm not shocked. Who are you engaged to?"

Kaden grinned. "I guess we did a good job at hiding our feelings. The thing is, I was worried about the age difference, but she didn't care and, well, it's Angie."

Lyra's mouth opened and closed, and then she grinned back. "How wonderful! I love her too." She launched herself at him with slightly less enthusiasm than Maggie had to Dan. "Congratulations! You two will be great together in so many ways."

Cinnamon leaped at the window behind them, barking madly. Lyra would have to go settle her whenever Kaden let her go.

"What?" Finn looked like someone who'd taken a large bite of a foul muffin but their mouth was too full now to say a word.

Lyra slid out of Kaden's arms and poked Finn in the chest. "When will you believe me about anything important? How many times do I have to tell you that Kaden is my best friend?"

He blinked rapidly. "But you said you love him."

"I do." She laughed at his confusion. "I love him as a good friend."

He shook his head, clearly unable to grasp the concept. "So, you don't care that he's marrying someone else?"

"Sheriff, you may be clever at police work, but you suck when it comes to understanding women."

"Considering he's never had a girlfriend, you may be right," Arabelle noted dryly.

Walker opened his mouth a few times, and since he was having such a hard time, Lyra jumped in to rescue him.

"I'm sure that's not true, and anyway we should be celebrating the happy couple and not the sheriff's shortcomings. I think this definitely calls for that champagne."

"That's my girl." Kaden winked at Walker, causing another scowl. "You really need to lighten up, Sheriff."

"Play nice, you two." Patricia put her arm on Finn's elbow. "We should talk."

A little nervous about what her mom's intentions might be, Lyra rustled up enough glasses. "Lucky there's not too many of us. A diner doesn't serve much champagne, so we don't have a lot of flutes. Let's do this outside."

"What about the customers?" Vanessa asked. "I'll stay out front."

Lyra shook her head. "No, we're celebrating together, and for once they can wait five minutes."

Cinnamon bounded around the group, happy to have plenty of people to pay her attention. Adept at it, Kaden opened the bottles so that corks flew across the veranda, accompanied by oohs as the champagne overflowed.

Lyra hugged the engaged couple. "I hope you'll allow me to cater the wedding?"

"Which one?" Maggie asked with a teasing glance at Kaden.

"Both."

"Hey, slow down," Kaden protested. "We just got engaged and certainly don't have a date yet."

"That's okay," Lyra said soothingly. "I'm just putting it out there, because when you do decide, I'll need more staff."

"What about us?" Vanessa sniffed.

"A wedding requires a lot more than all of us." Lyra chuckled. "Trust me, I've done a few."

"Oh, will it be big?" Earl crinkled his nose at what Lyra assumed was his first taste of champagne.

"Now, don't get carried away, Lyra. I'm not made of money," Dan pleaded.

"Besides, none of us have big families," Maggie added.

"I know that, but you do have a lot of people that love you. Unless I'm not allowed to say that, Sheriff?"

He had the good grace to smile. "You're not going to let me forget I said that, are you?"

"Never is a long time, so let's talk about it in ten years or so."

His eyes twinkled in the best way possible. "If that means you're staying in Fairview, then I guess I can handle it."

Now it was Lyra's turn to blush. It wasn't so much his words, although they were sweet. The way he said it with a little huskiness and looking deep into her eyes was what made her knees a little weak. "We have a deal."

From the corner of her eye, Lyra noticed Vanessa sneak back to work, and she locked eyes with Maggie, who was also smiling fondly with a hint of a question in those sparkling eyes.

"You know, I've been thinking about your lack of shows, and I wonder, once the dust has settled on

Raylene, if this isn't a good time to have a cooking contest? It might go a long way to getting the paparazzi to back off."

Lyra stared at her friend. "Or it might have the opposite effect by putting me back in the public eye."

"You do know this is hitting the news as we speak? You can't keep things like murder, attempted murder, and slander quiet. Not when the instigator owns a paper."

"Sure, but after all the effort I've put into laying low, we don't need to encourage it." Lyra put a hand up to forestall Maggie. "With the exception of the cookbook."

"Okay, but I think you'll find that paper will be dead in the water for a long time. Plus, if you did a contest locally, that would play things down. Double plus, maybe during it we'll find a few chefs who wouldn't cost a fortune, to work the weddings and any other events in the future."

Lyra shook her head fondly. "Mags, you always surprise me, even when I'd rather you didn't."

Her friend tilted her head and grinned. "I can't tell if you like the idea or not."

"It's brilliant. We wouldn't go as far as Portland, but if we visit towns south, west, and east of Fairview, that should net us a few good prospects. In fact, I've been dying to talk to a bakery owner in Maple Falls who won one of my competitions in New York a couple of years ago, then came back home. I've followed her achievements and she certainly has some talent. I bet there are more bakers and cooks like that out there."

Maggie snapped her fingers. "Country Cooking Collaborations."

"Ooh, nice!"

"Cupcake Cuties," Patricia called out on her way to help Vanessa.

"Hmm. What if men apply?" Lyra sipped her champagne as she pondered a new adventure so hot on the heels of something she'd rather forget.

"It could still work, but would they?" Maggie asked.

"Hello?" Kaden objected. "Some of the best bakers are men."

Maggie shrugged. "I suppose they might be cute."

"We could do with some of that around here."

"Mom!"

Patricia shrugged. "I'm not young, but I'm not dead. Some new blood in town would be nice is all I'm saying."

"Could we not use that word?" Earl implored.

"Dead?" Arabelle nodded. "You're right, son. We should toast the happy couples, but let's also send out some positive vibes for some boring days ahead."

Patricia snorted. "Have you met my daughter? She doesn't do boring."

The others laughed, including Lyra, but surprisingly her mind was already ticking over the cooking-competition idea. It always amazed her when Maggie had ideas that somehow linked to her plans. "I can see some travel in my future," she murmured.

"Me too." Kaden clinked her glass. "Just be careful out there."

Finn frowned. "We should talk about this."

"Not today, Sheriff," Lyra scolded gently. "Right now, let's savor the moment when we have nothing more important to do than enjoy good company."

The oven bell dinged loudly, and Lyra hurried to pull out a tray of savory muffins. There was still a diner to run amid the celebrations, and though muffins weren't exactly what went with champagne, these wouldn't make it into the diner. She placed them piping hot on a tray with butter in front of the team.

"Good timing." Maggie licked her lips. "I'm starving."

"They are pretty good." Finn grinned and helped himself to one, juggling it until it was cool enough to bite while Cinnamon caught the crumbs he dropped.

"Finally, you admit it. Cheers." Lyra clinked his glass.

He nodded and did likewise to Kaden and Dan. "Congratulations."

It wasn't exactly effusive, but at least it was a start.

Dan started talking about cars, and Kaden wandered off with him, leaving Lyra with Finn.

It took an effort to downplay the awkwardness. "Can I ask you what will happen to Raylene?"

He nodded. "She isn't off the hook by any means. The court case will decide if she's in any way responsible for Ardie's death, but I intend to put in a good word about her state of mind. Plus, there were no fingerprints on the knife, but the hair from the branch was Roman's, so I think she'll be okay."

"I know you're just doing your job, but thank you. She made some mistakes, only I don't think Ardie in that way was one of them."

"I shouldn't say this, but it will be common knowledge any day. Roman made some dodgy deals to raise capital for his plans to discredit you, and his paper will likely go under."

She let that sink in, then sighed. "I try never to gloat or wish somebody ill."

He raised an eyebrow. "But?"

"Let's just say I hope he and his son get the help they need, but I also hope he never gets to print another story about anyone ever again."

He smiled. "You can have your say in court to help make that happen."

"I'm not looking forward to that, but you can be sure I'll do my best."

His smile deepened. "You always do."

She blushed at the unexpected praise. "That's very kind of you."

"It's the truth. The way you care for your team is inspiring." Now he was a little red-cheeked. "Although it would be nice if you'd be more cautious in the future in how you go about that. In fact, I'm looking forward to a quieter time if you can stand it."

Finn was evolving into someone she truly admired. Or, she admitted to herself, maybe he'd always been this person, and she'd been too blind to see it. "I think that time for us without any drama would be heaven."

He smiled. "I like the sound of that."

"Come on, you two. Is this a celebration, or what?" Maggie called.

"I guess the quiet has to wait a while," Lyra said softly, hoping it wouldn't be too long, and by the way the clever beagle was hanging on Finn's every word, it seemed Cinnamon felt the same.

Thanks so much for reading Beagles Love Muffin But Murder Book 1 in the Beagle Diner Mystery series. I hope you enjoyed it!

If you did…

1 Help other people find this book by leaving a review.

2 Sign up for my new release e-mail, so you can find out about the next book as soon as it's available and receive the bonus epilogue! If you've previously joined, don't worry, you'll be able to get it very soon for free.

3 Come like my Facebook page.

4 Visit my caphipps.com for the very best deals.

5 Keep reading for an excerpt from the next book in the series, Beagles Love Layer Cake Lies

BEAGLES LOVE
LAYER CAKE LIES

Waving a sheaf of papers, Maggie demanded her attention. "The contestants will be arriving at the hotel soon."

Lyra checked her watch. "And?"

"You need to get down to the conference room there to greet them."

"Of course I do." There was plenty of time so Lyra pointed to her cup. "Can I enjoy the lull before the storm for five minutes first?"

"Sure, I just thought you might like to go over their applications before you go. You know, get a handle on who they are and why they entered the competition."

Lyra shrugged. "I already did that."

"Okay, but don't you want to brush up?" Maggie raised a perfect eyebrow. "You always used to pour over the applications for days."

"That was back when the shows were televised and the stakes were much higher for the contestants. This is a more laid-back affair and we'll have time to chat to each person without having to do extra takes that filming requires."

"It's a bit late for keeping it low-key, dear," mom told her. "The press have been here since yesterday, and I believe they are camped out at the hotel already."

"From what I've heard, this press group are nothing like what I experienced with the Paparazzi in LA. It will all be fine. Trust me."

Mom frowned. "Naturally, we all hope for the best, dear, but I agree with Maggie that we can't be too careful."

Lyra had just taken a large gulp of coffee when she caught the look between the other two and almost choked. "You mean with security? Why didn't either of you tell me you were worried?"

Mom and Maggie shared another look that Lyra couldn't decipher, but it was Maggie who spoke.

"We're not exactly worried. Not with Dan taking charge of it. We just want to be sure you stay safe."

When Lyra and Maggie first dreamed up the competition she'd considered stopping at the nearby towns and running a smaller one in each with a final in Fairview. After much thought she changed her mind. It involved too many issues with security and in truth she didn't want to be away from her business for months on end. Apparently, she wasn't worried enough—and that bothered her. Had she gotten complacent?

"You did say you had news, Mags. Do you know something I don't?"

Maggie blew a wayward dark curl off her face. "There have been a couple of items in the paper today. One was about reviews for some of the contestant's business's and they weren't flattering."

Lyra shrugged again. "It could be sour grapes on not getting a place in this competition. What was the other one about?"

"Apparently, one of the contestants, Scarlett Finch, has had a few run ins with the law in Cozy Hollow."

"What does that mean? We asked all the applicants if they had any criminal records on the application and they all said no. You were checking that, right?"

"That's true, I did check and she doesn't have any."

"Then I don't understand what's got you so anxious."

Maggie gave her a side-eye. "What concerns me is that she's not the only one."

"I assume you're talking about Madeline Flynn?"

"There has been a lot written about her in the Maple Falls paper and elsewhere."

"I know that, but the poor woman has my luck when it comes to crimes surrounding her, which you know about already, and with my history I certainly can't point a finger."

Mom snorted. "You can say that again."

Maggie rolled her eyes. "Look I just wanted you to know about my concerns. One would be bad enough, but two is asking for trouble."

"It's a little late to be discussing this when as you pointed out they're due to arrive in town at any minute. It's not like we can ax them now," Lyra huffed.

"She's just doing her job, dear."

"I know mom, and I do appreciate everything you do, Mags. Only, I thought you had exciting news and this is the complete opposite."

"Well," Maggie's frown was instantly replaced by a smirk, "I didn't mean to bring you down, and we were hoping that you're the one with news."

"Me?" Lyra was genuinely confused. "News about what?"

"How was the date?" Mom blurted clearly eager for the talk of the competition and contestant issues to finish.

Lyra should have known this was coming since Maggie had been thorough about the contestants. They had discussed Maddie Flynn in great depth and yet Lyra had walked into the trap like it had never happened before. "It was very nice, Mom." She avoided her mother's gaze and refilled Cinnamon's water bowl which didn't need it.

"Nice?" Mom snorted. "Pie is nice. Comfy shoes are nice. A date should be a little more than that, otherwise what's the point? Did he kiss you?"

"Mom!"

"What? A mother isn't allowed to inquire if the first man her daughter's dated in forever is up to standard?"

Lyra put her hand up. "Stop right now, or I will never date again."

Mom sniffed. "Fine. You two stay and chat. I'll head over to the diner and get started on breakfast for you. I know you'll want to check on things and I want to make sure you eat before you start your day."

"I won't be long," Lyra assured her, knowing that her mom would go straight there and inform her staff that the date was nice and wouldn't spare the sarcasm. This meant she would have to endure several innuendos and pointed questions, at the very least, from her mature staff members who couldn't help themselves.

The Diner was situated in front of the house and sat on Main Street, while her house's driveway was around the corner on a side road. A walkway into the parking lot between the two buildings made things easy, along with access via steps to a wide wooden veranda with French doors to enter the front of the diner, as well as the kitchen through a small hallway where the restrooms were situated.

Lyra employed several people who were competent enough, yet she liked to be hands on when she wasn't writing cookbooks or solving mysteries.

The latter came about by accident and more than once, hence her reputation. She had her fingers and toes crossed that from now on she was done with drama that didn't revolve around food—and that should also be kept at a minimum.

As soon as Mom was out of earshot, Maggie raised an eyebrow.

Lyra grimaced. "Let it go, Mags."

Maggie spouted. "My love life is an open book, which seems very one-sided in our friendship. You could at least say what happened on your date so I can pretend we're on equal footings."

"You and Dan are my best friends who I've known for years. It was pretty obvious to everyone else, if not the two of you, how you felt about each other. Finn and I are new, and we're taking things slow. If and when there is something to tell, you'll be the first to know."

"I better be," Maggie warned. She pushed the papers across to Lyra, tapping three of them. "Now, back to the contestants. I'm picking these will be the ones to watch."

Lyra sighed. It couldn't hurt to look over the details one more time if it kept Maggie out of her personal life.

Need to read more of <u>Beagles Love Layer Cake Lies</u> ?   Pick   up   your   copy   today!

RECIPES

These recipes are ones I use all the time and have come down the generations from my mum, grandmother, and some I have adapted from other recipes. Also, I now have my husband's grandmother's recipe book. Exciting! I'll be bringing some of them to life very soon.

Just a wee reminder, that I am a New Zealander. Occasionally I may have missed converting into ounces and pounds for my American readers.

My apologies for that, and please let me know—if you do try them—how they turn out.

Cheryl x

BANANA MUFFINS

Ingredients
1 3/4 cups flour
2 tsp baking powder
1/4 tsp baking soda
1/4 tsp salt
1/2 cup sugar
1 cup of mashed banana
2 eggs
1/4 cup milk
1/3 cup melted butter

Instructions
1 Heat oven to 180ºC or 350ºF
2 Sift flour baking soda and salt into a bowl.
3 Mix in sugar.
4 Melt butter and whisk with milk, bananas and eggs.
5 Add wet ingredients to dry and mix with a spatula.
6 Pour into muffin pans. (Makes 12)
7 Bake for 40 mins.

Cream Cheese Icing
1 cup confectioners sugar
1/4 cup butter
1/3 cup cream cheese
1 tablespoon lemon juice

Mix cream cheese and butter until smooth. Mix in confectioners sugar and then add enough lemon juice to make soft enough to spread on muffins.

Tips:

Add 1 cup chocolate chips to dry ingredients and mix in until coated in the flour so they don't sink in the mixture.

Great use of frozen bananas. (The ones that were going brown and you couldn't face eating them!)

Instead of frosting, slice in half and spread with butter.

OTHER BOOKS BY C. A. PHIPPS

Please note: Most are also available in paperback and some in audio.

Remember to join Cheryl's Cozy Mystery newsletter.

There's a free recipe book waiting for you. ;-)

Cheryl also writes romance as Cheryl Phipps.

BOOKS BY CHERYL PHIPPS

Women's Fiction

A New Life by Design

Listening for Love

Contemporary Romance

Billionaire Knights Series

Billionaire Knights Books 1-5

Restless Billionaire

Ruthless Billionaire

Reluctant Billionaire

Reckless Billionaire

Resident Billionaire

Millionaire - Family Ties Series

Millionaire - Family Ties Box Set 1-3

The Millionaire Next Door

The Millionaire's Proposal

The Millionaire's Seduction

Sycamore Springs Series

The Trouble With You and Me - Books 1-3

The Trouble with Friends

The Trouble with Exes

The Trouble with Love

Please note: most of these are available in paperback.

ABOUT THE AUTHOR

'Life is a mystery. Let's follow the clues together.'

C. A. Phipps is a USA Today best-selling author from beautiful New Zealand. Cheryl is an empty-nester living in a quiet suburb with her wonderful husband, 'himself'. With an extended family to keep her busy when she's not writing, there is just enough space for a crazy mixed breed dog who stole her heart! She enjoys family times, baking, and her quest for the perfect latte.

Check out her website http://caphipps.com
and her store https://caphippsstore.com

Made in United States
Orlando, FL
03 September 2024